Dear Reader,

I'm trying to remember what was going on in my life ten years ago when I wrote *Never Tease a Wolf*. Oddly enough, I got the idea for this book from an exhibit on the endangered gray wolf, which appeared in our local science museum. I took the brochure home with me because it mentioned a three-toed renegade wolf. I found a book on wolves and started reading. And thinking and wondering...

I ended up traveling to Big Timber, Montana, and talking to people in the sheep ranching business, which gave me a great deal of the background information I needed for this book and its companion, *A Wolf in Sheep's Clothing,* which will be reissued in 2002.

Because I've grown as a writer—and a person—over the past ten years, I've made some alterations in this edition of *Never Tease a Wolf* to reflect those changes. Enjoy!

Happy reading!

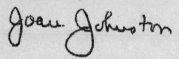

Also available from
JOAN JOHNSTON
and MIRA Books

A LITTLE TIME IN TEXAS

Coming June 2002

A WOLF IN SHEEP'S CLOTHING

JOAN JOHNSTON

Never Tease a Wolf

MIRA

ISBN 1-55166-805-X

NEVER TEASE A WOLF

Copyright © 1991 by Joan Mertens Johnston.

Visit us at www.mirabooks.com

Printed in U.S.A.

The facts about wolves at the opening of each chapter
are taken from the book *The Wolf: The Ecology and
Behavior of an Endangered Species* by L. David Mech,
and are reprinted by permission of the author.

I want to thank Ed Bangs, a wildlife biologist
with the U.S. Fish and Wildlife Service in Helena,
Montana, who provided me with information about the
Northern Rocky Mountain Wolf Recovery Plan,
and who kindly took me through the steps
for relocating a wolf under the plan.

And I especially want to thank my friend
Richard Wheeler, who spent a week in mid-May
driving me through snowstorms in and around
Big Timber, Montana, so I could get a good look
at the Boulder River Valley and the hot springs at Chico.
Your help was invaluable, Dick!

1

Wolves demonstrate aggressive behavior when meeting strange wolves.

Abigail Dayton saw a light on in the upper story of the old-fashioned wood-frame ranch house, so she knew there had to be someone there. But no one was answering her knock. She had an appointment to meet Luke Granger at 6:00 a.m. It was 5:55. He might be in one of the outbuildings, tending to his sheep, but she was betting he was still inside nursing a cup of hot coffee—something she could dearly use. April mornings could be quite frigid in the foothills of the Absaroka Mountains.

She tried the doorknob. Not surprisingly for this rural area of southwestern Montana, the door was unlocked. Abigail shoved the heavy oak door open and took a hesitant step inside.

"Hello? Agent Dayton, Fish and Wildlife Service. Anybody home?"

She heard the rattle of pans and a virulent curse and followed the noise toward the back of the house, where golden light streamed from an open doorway.

There was nothing remotely feminine about the living room she passed through, which contained a mounted twelve-point elk head over the fieldstone fireplace and huge pieces of wood-and-rawhide furniture centered on a Navajo rug. The picture windows overlooking the snow-capped Absarokas were bare of frilly curtains—or any kind of curtains, for that matter.

Abigail carefully stepped over several farm and ranch journals, a plaid western shirt with pearl snaps and a crumpled beer can that littered the hardwood floor.

She stopped abruptly in the doorway to what turned out to be the kitchen, not believing the fascinating picture she beheld.

On the worn linoleum floor sat a broad-shouldered, long-legged man with three lambs in his lap. He was trying desperately to balance three bottles of formula in three eagerly sucking mouths. Dark lashes lay against his sun-browned cheeks, and shaggy black hair fell across his forehead nearly to his thick black brows.

A stubble of dark beard shadowed his face, which was thin, almost gaunt, with cheekbones that appeared even higher because of the sunken hollows beneath them. His mouth was wide, but his lips were thin, almost severe. She wouldn't have called him handsome. Striking, maybe.

However, it wasn't his face that drew her attention, but his hands. They were large and work-worn, with a sprinkle of black hair across the knuckles. Powerful hands, performing a delicate task with utmost gentleness.

His low voice modulated from silky to harsh and back again as he alternately crooned to the lambs and swore at them. But his touch stayed slow and easy. Those were hands that would know how to caress a woman.

Abigail was startled by the direction of

her thoughts. She'd been alone since her husband Sam's accidental death three years before. The rancher's tenderness with the lambs reminded her how much she missed having a man hold her in his arms. She repressed the feelings of loss and pain, forcing herself to focus on the reason she had come here.

"You look like you could use another hand," she said.

The rancher's head jerked up at the sound of her voice, and his fierce gray eyes narrowed as he stared at her. "Who the hell are you? What are you doing here?"

Abigail bristled. "I'm Agent Dayton, Fish and Wildlife. *You* called *me*—or rather, the Service. I have an appointment with you this morning."

He raised a questioning brow. "They sent a woman?"

"You have a problem with that?" she asked, tensing for a fight.

"Nope. Especially since I won't be needing your services after all. So you can take yourself right back where you came from, Agent Dayton."

Abigail didn't like the rancher's tone of voice and wasn't about to accept his abrupt dismissal. "What happened to the wolf you sighted—the one you called about—that I'm here to catch and relocate before it kills any of your sheep?"

"You're too late."

"Too late?"

"Why do you think I'm sitting here with these three bum lambs? Damned renegade killed two of my sheep yesterday. I phoned your office to cancel our appointment late yesterday afternoon."

Abigail groaned. She'd left the office in Helena at noon yesterday and spent the night at a bed-and-breakfast in Big Timber, a tiny town halfway between Bozeman and Billings, so she could be here in the Boulder River Valley on time this morning.

"I've got a call in to Animal Damage Control to handle the problem," he said. "Now get out."

Abigail's mouth thinned into a bitter line. Animal Damage Control, a division of the U.S. Department of Agriculture, could—and would—use "lethal measures" to dispose of any wolf that killed livestock. Fish and Wildlife was fighting a losing battle with its recovery program, devoted to saving the gray wolf, which was an endangered species. It was especially difficult when most wolf habitat bordered on sheep and cattle ranges. She could understand the rancher's concerns, but she was angered by the quickness with which "relocation" had been abandoned in favor of "elimination."

She made a decision then and there to change Luke Granger's mind. There was no reason why she shouldn't have a chance to catch and relocate that wolf. With the sophisticated radio-tracking collars the Service was using now, she could keep an eye on the renegade, and if it ever threatened Granger's sheep again, she would put the animal down herself.

Abigail squared her shoulders and lifted her chin, preparing to do battle.

"Look," she said. "You're going to get reimbursed by that private environmental organization, the Defenders of Wildlife, for the two sheep you lost—assuming it doesn't turn out to be a coyote that killed them. In that case, of course, you're responsible for the loss. But—''

''I know wolf sign when I see it,'' the rancher interrupted. ''This renegade has a three-toed right forefoot. Probably lost the fourth toe in a trap. And big. I've got plenty of wolf sign, all right. Tracks and bite marks and scat.''

''Maybe there are extenuating circumstances. Maybe—''

''Maybe you should get your cute little butt out of here.''

Abigail felt her cheeks heating with a combination of anger and embarrassment as his eyes roamed up her jean-clad legs toward her derriere. She rued the fact that her sheepskin-lined denim jacket ended at her waist.

His eyes deepened to a smoky gray and focused on her primmed mouth as he drawled, ''Or maybe you'd like to hang around and—''

''Now, you look here, Mr. Granger. I—''

''Luke. You know, I'm kinda partial to green-eyed gals. 'Specially ones with pretty blond hair like yours. How long is it, anyway? Can't tell the way you have it all hitched up on top of your head like that.''

''We are not discussing—''

Suddenly he wasn't on the floor anymore, he was standing up across from her. The lambs began bleating frantically. Abigail knew exactly how they felt.

Luke Granger took a step toward her. Abigail was determined to hold her ground, but he was a head taller than she and standing so close to him was disconcerting. She could feel his body heat, almost see the muscles rippling under the plaid wool shirt stretched across his broad chest. His jeans fit like a second skin, leaving little—and there was nothing little about him—to the imagination.

His moist breath fanned her face, causing goose bumps to rise on her arms. Abigail took a step backward—and tripped over one of the lambs.

''Whoa, there,'' the rancher said as he reached out to catch her. ''Can't have you bruising that cute little—''

''Don't say it!'' Abigail hissed.

The rancher tightened his hold to keep

them both from falling, pulling her breasts up flush with his chest and her belly into the V created by his spread legs, thus capturing her hands at her sides.

Abigail felt a surge of desire so strong it frightened her. She stared with awe at the rugged face of the man who had her trapped in his arms. A suffocating fear surfaced, surprising her because she had no idea of its source. She only knew she had to get free. *Now.*

"Listen, Mr. Granger, I don't know what you think you're doing, but—"

His hand snagged the clip holding her hair on top of her head and released it. Honey-blond waves swirled down around her shoulders. He sifted his fingers through the silky mass. "Beautiful," he murmured.

Abigail shivered with pleasure. "Let me go, Mr. Granger," she said in a calm, rational, but disgracefully breathless, voice.

Luke knew he ought to let her go. But it wasn't that simple. He'd only taken her in his arms to keep her from falling on her fanny. But once she was there, her lithe figure aligned with his, he hadn't been able to resist the urge to release that clip in her hair.

He hadn't expected the fierce rush of heat between them, hadn't expected his body to tauten with need. He wanted her in a way he hadn't wanted a woman in a long time. He wanted to feel her naked beneath him, wanted to feel their heated bodies—

"Mr. Granger, I..." Abigail's voice faded as she recognized the raw heat in the rancher's eyes. It was both thrilling and terrifying. Her breath came in panting gasps and her pulse speeded. She saw the question in his eyes. It would take only one word from her to unleash that fierce desire. But she couldn't make herself say it.

Luke swore softly and fluently under his breath. The look in her eyes, her pulse and her trembling body all signaled that she shared his feelings. She hadn't said no, but she wasn't saying yes, either. He'd never taken anything from a woman she didn't willingly offer, and he wasn't about to start now. Nevertheless, when she shifted slightly in his arms, instead of releasing her, he tightened his grasp.

"I'd like to leave now," she said.

"I gave you a chance to leave," he said in a harsh voice. "You chose to stay."

Abigail wasn't prone to panic. But things were getting decidedly out of hand. She was an expert at setting traps, but this was the first time in recent history she could remember getting caught in one. And the trapped feeling was only getting worse. She knew she couldn't let this go any further. Well, there were not-so-civilized ways to handle Neanderthals like Luke Granger.

"I am an agent for the United States government, here on official business. You lay one hand on me—" Abigail gasped as his hand lifted her chin and slowly angled her face up toward his "—and I will…"

Her wide green eyes met his lambent gaze. His mouth lowered. Abigail gasped when Luke's lips met hers with a brief touch, a halting taste.

"You taste sweet, woman," he said in a husky voice.

Abigail stiffened, to keep from melting in his arms. "I'm warning you—"

Luke's mouth came searching again. His

touch, his taste, combined to seduce her. Abigail tensed as she felt the heat pooling in her belly. But along with the thrill, the fear returned. She had to stop him. She lifted her booted foot, aiming for his instep.

But a strong hand grasped her thigh and held it tight, thwarting her intention.

Startled, Abigail looked up into a pair of rueful eyes.

"That would have hurt," he said.

"That was the general idea," she retorted.

He didn't let go of her thigh right away, just held it nestled against his own, letting the heat build between them.

Finally she said, "You can—" Her voice cracked. She cleared her throat and repeated, "You can let me go now."

Slowly, ever so slowly, Luke let her thigh slide down his leg to the floor, his eyes never leaving hers, so he saw the renewed flare of desire she couldn't hide. And her surprise and confusion at what had happened between them.

What had happened, anyway? he wondered. It had started out innocently—he had reached out to keep her from falling—but somewhere along the line, other needs had taken precedence. He had no explanation for his behavior. But here he stood, fully and painfully aroused by an agent for the Fish and Wildlife Service! It was hard to say which of them was more upset by the encounter.

It was time he called a halt to this thing—whatever it was—that had flared between them.

Luke looked hard at the woman standing across from him, trying to discern what it was about her that had attracted him. He was baffled. There was something about her green eyes, maybe it was the way they slanted at the corners, that reminded him of a sleek feline animal.

A lot of women he knew reminded him of cats, soft and clingy and inclined to purr when you rubbed them in the right places. But once they got their claws into a man, they never let go.

He noted that Agent Dayton—he knew her by no other name—also had flawless peach skin that rose over wide cheekbones, a no-nonsense nose, and a chin that had been upraised in challenge since the moment he'd laid eyes on her.

Her lips were extraordinary. Full and lusciously pink, they virtually disappeared into a thin line when she was angry. Right now they were pursed. Pouty. Kissable. He couldn't regret kissing her, but he wasn't pleased that he'd succumbed so totally to her allure.

"You'll be needing this," he said at last, retrieving her hair clip from his shirt pocket where he had tucked it and handing it to her. "You'd better get going if you're going."

She stuck the clip in her front jeans pocket without trying to fix her hair. "If I can have just a moment of your time—"

"I thought you were in a hurry to leave?"

"I have a favor to ask first."

"You sure have a funny way of asking for favors, Agent Dayton." He walked over to pick up a bottle that one of the lambs had nudged into a corner. "If I hadn't stopped you in time, I'd be limping on a bruised instep right now.''

She avoided his accusing look, staring instead at the pitifully bleating lambs.

''I think we're going to need a little more peace and quiet to talk,'' Luke said. ''Grab a bottle.''

She dropped to her knees, collared a lamb and offered it a bottle. Luke followed suit with the other two lambs, and when all three lambs were once again sucking greedily, he prompted, ''I'm listening.''

''I want you to let me capture the wolf that attacked your sheep, instead of sending for Animal Damage Control.''

''No.''

''Why not?''

''I can't afford to lose any more sheep,'' Luke said.

''That's a poor argument. The Defenders of Wildlife will reimburse you for any sheep you lose to a wolf.''

''*If* I can prove it was a wolf did the killing. But you know, and I know, Agent Dayton, that I may not find some of those wolf-slaughtered sheep for a while. And when I do, there may not be enough of the carcass left to know what killed them. Then I'm out the price of a spring wool shearing, or a lamb sold for slaughter in the fall.''

He saw from the look on her face that she wasn't ready to concede defeat.

''Doesn't it bother you to be responsible for the death of an animal that's an endangered species?'' she asked.

His brow furrowed before he said, ''That's not the point.''

''That's precisely the point,'' she argued. ''Unless individuals like you are willing to help, we haven't got a prayer of recovering wolves in Montana.''

''Maybe the wolf's day is done. Maybe they ought to be extinct.''

''You can't believe that!'' she said in a shocked voice.

One of Luke's lambs had emptied its bottle and wandered off to the pallet in the corner of the kitchen that had become the lambs' bed. Luke used his free hand to scratch the shadow of whiskers under his chin. ''Wolves are a menace to stock.''

''If you're going to use that rationale for

letting the wolf become extinct, you might as well exterminate every other animal that becomes inconvenient to have around,'' she said, green eyes flashing.

Luke flushed. "What about survival of the fittest?"

"What about it?" she challenged. "Surely you aren't going to suggest that wolves are endangered because they haven't evolved to survive in their environment. All wolves really need to survive nowadays are hides impervious to bullets and stomachs that can handle poison.''

Luke had opened his mouth to retort when they were interrupted by the entrance of a wiry little man wearing jeans, a quilted vest, plaid shirt, cowboy boots and a baseball cap fringed by wisps of gray hair.

"Didn't know you had company, Luke. I'll just take myself back outside—''

"Wait a minute, Shorty." Luke carefully lifted the slumbering lamb out of his lap and settled it on the pallet in the corner of the kitchen next to the other one. "The lady isn't 'company.' This is Agent Dayton from Fish and Wildlife.''

Shorty chortled. "Well, can you beat that? They got females doing purty near everything these days."

As soon as Luke lifted the lamb out of his visitor's lap, she scrambled to her feet and held out her hand to the old man.

"Hi. Abigail Dayton."

Shorty stared at her hand for a moment. Then he took off his cap with his left hand, exposing a bald head, and dragged his right palm across his jeans to wipe it off before extending it to her. "Shorty Benton. Pleased to meet you, ma'am."

"Please call me Abigail."

Luke's mouth curved in a wry grin. "She's had me calling her Agent Dayton all morning. What's your secret, Shorty?"

"I mind my manners," Shorty said. "Which is more than I can usually say for you. You offered this young lady any coffee yet?"

Luke sheepishly shook his head no.

"Well, that's your problem, see," Shorty said as he headed for the stove. "Can't hardly 'spect someone to be civil this hour of the morning if she ain't been offered a cup of coffee. You want some coffee, Miss Abigail?''

"I'd love a cup."

Before Luke could count to five, he and Abigail were seated across from each other at a quaint wooden kitchen table with a mug of hot, black coffee in front of each of them, and Shorty was cooking up some eggs and bacon on the ancient gas stove.

"Shorty's sort of a fixture around here," Luke said.

"Are you two family?" Abigail asked.

"Near enough," Shorty said. "I've diapered that boy's bottom."

The warm, husky sound of Abigail Dayton's laughter sent a shiver of pleasure rolling down Luke's spine.

"'Spect Luke told you that wolf he sighted done killed some sheep," Shorty said as he expertly flipped a fried egg.

"He told me. I've been trying to convince him to let me capture the wolf anyway," Abigail said.

"S'pose he weren't too hot on the idea. Luke can be a right stubborn cuss."

Luke shifted in his chair, trying to find a

more comfortable position without disturb-
ing the lamb that had left the comfort of the
pallet and settled its head on his thigh.

"Maybe I haven't been using the right
arguments. What would you suggest?"
Abigail focused her gaze on Shorty, and
Luke watched the old man turn to mush at
the pleading look in her big green eyes.

"How 'bout it, Luke?" Shorty asked.
"You gonna give the lady a chance to catch
that wolf?"

"Stay out of this, Shorty," Luke warned.

Shorty watched the hairs come up on
Luke's neck. It was plain as a wart on your
nose that Luke didn't want to spend no time
with Abigail Dayton. But Shorty had seen
the sparks flying when he'd found the two
of them sitting on the floor together.

Luke might not want to be attracted to
the lady, but he was. Which was a surprise
in itself, because Abigail weren't Luke's
type. Oh, he liked blondes, all right. But
they usually had a might more curvy bodies
and went in for a lot of face paint and fancy
clothes. And they all knew the score. Miss
Abigail was likely a babe in the woods by

comparison. To Shorty's way of thinking, she was exactly what Luke needed.

In the ten years since his divorce, Luke hadn't spent more than a month or two with a woman before she was out of his life. Shorty grimaced. That boy wasn't going to let any woman get too close. Not after the examples set by his mama and his ex-wife.

No, if Luke had his way, Miss Abigail and her pleading green eyes would be out the front door before the sun was fully up. Shorty had to make sure that didn't happen.

"I 'spect, Luke, you better take Miss Abigail up on her offer."

"Why is that?" Luke asked cautiously.

"'Cause I just recalled them sheep was killed by coyotes. Yep. Coyotes. And when some official comes nosing around asking questions, so's to fill in all them claim forms, that's what I'm gonna say."

"You old piece of wolf bait! You say that and I'm going to have to eat the loss on those sheep. You wouldn't dare!"

Shorty served two perfect, over-easy eggs onto Luke's plate and added a half dozen strips of bacon. He grinned, exposing tobacco-stained teeth, and said, "Try me."

Luke fumed silently while he made short work of his breakfast. Shorty would do it, too. But he wasn't about to let that old reprobate manipulate him into doing something he didn't want to do. Unfortunately he wasn't immune to Abigail Dayton's pleading eyes either. The woman's arguments were getting to him. Not that he intended to let her know that. Once you let a woman get the upper hand, it was all over but the crying. He wasn't about to let Abigail Dayton find out she had any influence whatsoever on his decisions.

But maybe he'd been a bit hasty calling Animal Damage Control. If Agent Dayton was good at her job, it wouldn't take them long to trap that renegade wolf.

He sneaked a peek at her face, surprised to find a look of anxiety and hopeful expectation. It would take a real bastard to disappoint a face like that. Luke might be a lot of unsavory things, but a bastard wasn't one of them. Although, knowing his mama, it was mere luck that he wasn't.

"All right," he said quietly.

"Does that mean you're going to let me catch the wolf?" Abigail said, her eyes full of hope.

"I'll give you three days."

"Ten."

"All right, a week," he conceded.

Her jaw jutted, and she shook her head. "Ten days."

Any other woman would have compromised, Luke thought. He was being damned generous to let her trap the wolf in the first place. But he could see she wasn't going to back down. Hell, if she couldn't do it in a week, he could. It wouldn't be any skin off his nose to give her what she wanted. "Ten days," he agreed.

From the smile that lit her face you'd have thought he'd said the wolf could just help itself to all the sheep it wanted, and he wouldn't complain.

"You won't be sorry," she said. "I'm good at what I do. It may take me more than a week, but—"

"I'll make sure it doesn't," he said. "Because I'm going with you."

Her emerald eyes flashed with irritation

that she quickly concealed. "I appreciate your offer to help, Mr. Granger. But I work alone."

"Not on my land, you don't," he said in a hard voice.

Luke watched her lips thin into an angry line, while a flush turned her cheeks from peach to rose.

"Of course I can't stop you from coming along," she said in a carefully controlled voice. "But don't you have other things you need to do?"

"No need to worry about that," Shorty piped up. "I can handle things around here while Luke's busy with you."

Luke watched as Abigail Dayton shot a disapproving glance at Shorty that sent him scurrying for the door.

"I got some things need finished 'fore the day's done," the old man said.

When she turned her gaze back on Luke, he smiled like a wolf with a juicy lamb in its teeth. "Either I go with you, or you don't go. Make up your mind which it's going to be."

Her hands curled like she was itching to

get at his throat. She quickly stuffed them into the back pockets of her jeans and said in a terse voice, "Get your coat, Mr. Granger. The daylight's wasting."

2

Individual wolves can differ greatly.

"As long as you're coming along with me, you might as well make yourself useful," Abigail said as she settled into the worn leather seat of her battered pickup. "Where did the wolf depredations occur? That's the best place to pick up the trail. Oh, and the passenger door—"

Luke was already settling in on the other side of the bench seat by the time Abigail finished "—is hard to get open." Obviously not so for a man used to working with his hands. Abigail realized suddenly that the hands she'd seen being so gentle with the lambs must also be quite strong.

"Head for the East Boulder road," Luke said, gesturing out the open window in the direction he wanted her to take. "I lease land up in the mountains from the government. My sheep graze there once it warms up.''

Abigail shivered as the brisk wind turned her cheeks red. ''This is warmed up?''

''May is only a few days off. It's been warmer this year than usual—an early spring. Maybe I'm taking a chance thinking there won't be any more snow, but there's already grass on the mountains, so I'm willing to risk it.''

It was easy to see how Sweet Grass County, which encompassed the Boulder River Valley, had gotten its name. The valley was covered with a carpet of rich, bright green, most of which was feed that had been planted by sheepmen, Abigail conceded. But she could imagine it mantled with knee-deep grass, as it must have been when the first mountain men had come here. The Boulder River, its banks lined with towering cottonwoods, sparkled on a meandering course down the center of the valley, which eased into mountainsides covered by darker green juniper and jack pines.

Abigail turned off the narrow two-lane

highway onto a dirt-and-gravel road that followed the east tributary of the Boulder River up into the mountains. Mule deer and elk abounded. It was unfortunate the wolf hadn't stayed with its primary prey instead of feeding on Luke Granger's sheep.

Wolves generally ran in packs, and it was important to separate a wolf that had started hunting stock because it was likely to encourage other pack members to the same behavior.

Luke had labeled this wolf a renegade—meaning it hunted alone. "Are you sure this is a solitary wolf?" Abigail said. "Not part of a breeding pair? Or a pack, maybe?"

"None of the sheepmen I know have sighted any wolves this spring," he said. "Or found any wolf sign. The three-toed monster I saw might have been half of a breeding pair. I have no way of knowing that. If so, the female would be denned up with her pups this time of year."

"If you had her mate killed, the pups would go hungry," Abigail pointed out.

The male wolf making a kill would swallow as much as he could and return to the den. When the pups licked the wolf's mouth and nose, it would regurgitate food for the pups to eat. Thus, no father, no food.

"I'm not running a wolf farm here," Luke said. "I raise sheep."

Abigail kept her mouth shut, despite the urge to argue, and spent the rest of the drive up into the mountains in silence. She took advantage of the time to enjoy the beauty of the sun and open sky, and the colorful wildflowers—Dodge willow, columbine and purple crazyweed—gracing the mountainsides.

"Stop up there, where you see the break in the forest," Luke said. "There's a trail."

Abigail pulled the pickup off to the side of the road.

"We'll have to hike from here," Luke said.

Abigail could tell from the way he looked askance at her, that he expected a protest. But she was wearing sturdy walking boots and had her gear packed so she could carry it on her back all day if necessary. On more than one occasion, she had.

"You need any help with that?" he

asked when she hefted her pack onto her shoulders.

Abigail smiled and said, "I'm fine. Lead on."

Luke caught himself staring at the beauty of her smile and jerked his head away. She didn't fool him. When a woman smiled, he'd learned to beware. She usually wanted something. Sometimes his money. Sometimes his body. But there wasn't an unselfish bone in a one of them, at least, not that he'd seen.

He took off into the forest at a rate intended to tire her in a hurry, so she would see this wasn't going to work. But half an hour later, when he reached the site where the wolf had killed his sheep, she was right behind him. And she wasn't even breathing hard.

"Here they are," he said gruffly as he pulled a tarp off two dead sheep. "I did what I could to preserve the evidence until somebody could confirm what I found."

Abigail slipped the pack off her back onto the ground and knelt beside the remains of two white Rambouillet sheep. The impression of a three-toed wolf paw had dried in the earth beside the larger of the two ewes. The paw print alone wasn't proof of a wolf kill. A coyote could have made the kill, and a wolf might have come along and feasted on the carrion.

She turned to the other sheep and found the proof she needed. There was only one wound on the sheep. To be certain, she measured, but the diameter of the bite was too big to be that of a coyote.

"This was done by a wolf, all right," she admitted with a sigh. "How did you find the carcasses?"

"I was out riding and flushed a bunch of ravens and magpies. When I came to take a look, this is what I found."

Abigail began asking all the questions necessary to confirm that Luke Granger was entitled to reparation for the loss of his sheep. The form she filled out would be forwarded to the environmental group so they could determine whether, and how much, to pay the rancher.

"Any livestock carcasses around that might be considered attractants?"

Luke stuck his hands into his back pockets, stretching the fabric tight enough that Abigail suddenly found the ground at her feet very interesting. "I bury my dead lambs, Agent Dayton. I don't leave them in a stack behind the barn to attract wolves."

"Then you're the exception to the rule," Abigail replied tartly, her head snapping up and her eyes seeking out the rancher's face.

The muscles in his jaw were working, and Abigail was sure he wanted to say more. But he didn't.

Abigail ran a hand through her hair and looked around to see if she could find which way the wolf had traveled. "What kind of terrain will we find in that direction?" she asked at last.

"More of the same. There's a creek that runs down the mountain about a mile off."

From long practice, Abigail had learned that she had more luck catching a wolf if she set her traps in places where the wolf was likely to go: a crossroad between two deer trails; any place near water where there were wolf tracks; a moose or elk feeding spot; and, of course, the site of the kill.

"I need to locate some spots for my traps. You ready to do some more walking?"

"I'm at your command," Luke responded with a tip of his Stetson. He opened his mouth to offer again to help her with the pack, but she already had it on her back and was heading off through the forest. He shrugged and followed her. Miss Abigail Dayton was a grown woman. If she wanted help, he was sure she would ask for it.

Abigail had a great deal of stamina, and she was in excellent physical shape, but the pack was heavy, and the mountain terrain was grueling. But she would choke before she asked Luke Granger to share the load. He'd made it clear he didn't think a woman could handle the job. Well, she would show him!

At first she was glad Luke wasn't the talkative type. One of the best parts of her job was spending time like this, quiet time outdoors, where working was a joy. After a while, her curiosity got the better of her. She wanted to know more about Luke Granger. It was obvious he wasn't going to volunteer any information about himself.

So as she pulled on her gloves and spread a ground cloth at the first of the sites she had found to put a steel-jawed leg-hold trap, she asked, "How long have you been in the sheep ranching business?"

He gave her a sidelong glance, but finally answered, "All my life. This place was my father's and my grandfather's and his father's before him. How long have you been tracking wolves?"

"Two years." Abigail finished carefully winding a ten-foot-long drag chain that was attached to the trap into the hole she had dug. "Before that I was a park ranger stationed in northwestern Montana with my—" Abigail set the opened trap on top of the chain and covered it with a piece of waxed paper, careful not to get any human scent on anything.

"With your what?" he prodded.

"My husband."

Luke drew in a harsh breath at that surprising bit of information. "You're married."

"A widow."

Her eyes met his, and there was such a wealth of suffering and sadness there that he wanted to take her into his arms. There were other feelings that kept him from doing it—inexplicable feelings of jealousy for a man she still mourned and the knowledge that only a fool would ask for the kind of pain that inevitably came along with caring for a woman.

"What happened to your husband?"

"Grizzly attack."

That was unusual enough that Luke knew he must have heard about it at the time. Then he remembered. "I read about that—three years ago. Some hikers were lost in the forest at Glacier National Park, and the park ranger went in after them. The hikers were toting a grizzly cub they'd found. The ranger caught up to them about the same time as the cub's mother. He saved their lives—and lost his own. Am I right?"

She nodded. Tears had welled in her eyes, and she brushed them away with her sleeve and continued sifting dirt over the waxed paper to conceal the trap, blending in some pine needles to make the spot look more natural.

"He must have been quite a man," Luke said quietly.

"He was," Abigail replied. "Sam and I were childhood sweethearts. We went all through high school and college together. I married him my senior year after my—"

Luke waited for her to finish her sentence, and realized that it must be another case of something else hurtful in her past. "After what?" he asked gently.

She looked up again, and he saw more of the anguish he'd found before. "After my parents were killed in a plane crash. My father was the pilot, and my mother was with him because they always went everywhere together. He was heading down to Colorado to look at some bulls—I was raised on a cattle ranch near Bozeman—and something went wrong. They never did find out what caused the crash. Mom and Dad were killed instantly." Or at least, that was what Abigail had made herself believe. She couldn't bear the thought of her parents suffering— like she knew Sam had. "They died as

much in love, after twenty-two years together, as they were the day they married.''

Abigail estimated about sixteen inches
forward from the trap and put down a few
drops of a gland lure called Widow Maker.
If everything worked as it should, when the
wolf stepped forward to sniff at the lure, his
foreleg would land in the trap.

Once the wolf started running, the ten-
foot chain would follow, and the curved
hook at the end of the chain would catch
on a bit of brush or a dead log and stop
him. Without a firm hold to pull against, the
wolf wouldn't be able to tear off its foot
trying to escape the trap.

When she checked the traps she would
be able to locate the wolf by following the
trail left by the dragging chain. She would
use a tranquilizer dart, then cage the wolf
for relocation. The steel jaws of the trap
were still slightly separated when closed
and would leave minor puncture wounds
that healed in a matter of days.

It wasn't a perfect system, but it was the
best they'd been able to devise.

Abigail was brought from her reverie by the sound of Luke's voice.

"That must have been traumatic for you. To lose your parents. And then your husband."

"As you can see, I survived." *Barely.* It had been awful, at age twenty-one, to lose her parents. It had been catastrophic, at a mere twenty-three, to lose her husband. Sam had been more than her lover; he had been her best friend. It had been terrifying to be ripped from a warm, loving cocoon and thrust out into the cold, cruel world to make her way alone.

At first, she'd wanted to die herself. Once the initial shock and horror of Sam's death had passed, she hadn't been able to find the courage to stop living. Instead, she'd donned the necessary protective layers to defend herself, and she'd survived. But nothing about the past three years had been easy.

Abigail stood and carefully removed the ground cloth she'd used so there would be no human scent near the trap. "One down, three to go."

Once she'd collected everything in her pack, she set out again.

Despite the feeling that he was making a big mistake not to leave Agent Dayton to her business—at which she was quite good and extremely efficient—and get back to his own, Luke came up off his haunches and followed her.

When he'd caught up to her, and they were walking side by side, he asked, "Do you have any children?" Luke didn't know why he'd asked the question, it had just popped out.

She ducked a juniper branch, then said, "No. Sam and I wanted to wait and spend some time just enjoying each other. We thought we had plenty of time."

Her wan smile touched something inside Luke that he'd thought was encased in solid stone. It sure was a good thing she wasn't his type. Because he was pretty certain no man was ever going to measure up to a heroic figure like Sam Dayton.

"What about you?" Abigail asked. "Have you ever been married?"

"Once," Luke replied curtly. "That was enough."

"How long ago was that?"

"I've been divorced for ten years. And I don't want to talk about it."

Abigail clucked her tongue. "Must have been quite a woman to put such a lasting burr under your saddle."

"She was a two-timing bitch, with one hand on my wallet and the other hand on my—"

"Your what?" Abigail prompted.

"My privates," he said, using the least offensive word he could find. He smiled sardonically when even that word caused Abigail to flinch. He dropped a little behind her so he could watch the interesting way her hips moved under the weight of her pack.

"So you've sworn off women as a result?" she asked.

"Sworn off marrying them, anyway," he said.

"All women aren't like you describe your wife."

"Could have fooled me."

"I find it very sad that you've condemned yourself to living alone the rest of your life because of one bad experience."

"If you're so hot on marriage, why haven't you remarried?"

She smiled at him over her shoulder, and he felt his chest constrict.

"That's simple," she said, focusing her attention back on the trail in front of her. "I haven't found a man I could love as much as I loved Sam Dayton."

"And never will," Luke muttered under his breath.

Abigail stopped in her tracks and turned to confront him. "What did you say?"

"You obviously heard me the first time."

"I heard you. I just didn't believe what I heard. If I found a man I could love as much as Sam, I'd be married like *that!*" She snapped her fingers. "I loved being married. I loved being in love. I *want* to be married and have children and enjoy the comfort and companionship of—"

"That kind of happily-ever-after only happens in fairy tales," Luke interrupted harshly. "You're remembering the good

stuff, and forgetting all the bad, because of
how he died. You—"

"How *dare* you say I didn't have a good
marriage! Sam loved me. And I loved him.
We—"

"Probably never had an argument in
your lives," Luke said.

"We didn't!"

Luke snorted in disbelief.

"Or maybe we did," Abigail conceded,
shoving her hair away from her face in irritation. "But they were honest arguments
where we addressed our differences and settled them. We didn't let them fester and become big problems. We were friends. Can't
you understand that?"

Luke shook his head. "No, I can't. My
mother and father... Hell, you don't want
to hear the sordid story of my childhood."

Abigail put a hand on his arm to keep
him from walking away. "I do. I do want
to hear."

Luke felt something shift inside as he met
her sympathetic gaze. Against his better
judgment, he found himself telling her
about his mother. "She never loved her

husband. Or her son. She only loved her-self.''

And other men. And my father's money.

''I used to wonder why my father ever married her. Until I fell in love for the first time myself. Then I understood how it hap-pened. Because, God help me, I'd chosen to love a woman who was no better than my mother.

''My parents never divorced,'' Luke con-tinued in a bitter voice. ''They lived to-gether in misery for twenty-five long years. They went to an anniversary party a neigh-bor held for them, but they never made it home over some icy mountain roads. I heard later that my mother had made an em-barrassing scene at the party, saying she didn't know why she'd stayed with him all those years. She didn't know what they were celebrating. She felt like she'd spent twenty-five years in hell.''

Luke's bleak eyes met Abigail's horrified gaze. ''I still don't know if it was an acci-dent, or whether my father drove over the edge of that snowy mountain on purpose.''

Her grip tightened on Luke's arm in an

attempt to offer some support, but he shrugged it off.

"Anyhow, I came to my senses after I'd been married for a while and saw that my wife was just as unhappy and unsatisfied as my mother had been. I made up my mind I wasn't going to spend the next twenty-five years being miserable and maybe end up driving us both over a cliff. So I divorced her. And I haven't had the least inclination since to set myself up to endure a fiasco like that again."

"I'm so sorry," Abigail said.

Luke's gray eyes blazed with anger. "I don't want or need your pity!"

"It's not pity, exactly," Abigail said as she turned away and knelt to set another trap. "It's just that, once you've been loved by someone as I've been loved, totally and without reservation, you want everyone else to experience the same thing."

"I've learned my lesson," Luke said. "I'm not going to make the same mistake twice."

"Not even if you found a woman who

loved you?" Abigail said in a soft voice. "I mean *really* loved you?"

"How can you tell the real thing when you see it?" Luke questioned with a cynical twist of his mouth. "I don't believe I've ever seen the genuine article. Are you sure it even exists?"

"Oh, it exists all right."

Looking at her radiant face, Luke had to believe she was telling the truth—at least as she saw it. "So do you think you're ever going to find another man to love who's as perfect as Sam Dayton?"

"I honestly don't know," Abigail admitted.

"Are you even going to try?" Luke asked, an edge in his voice.

Abigail frowned at him. "Not that it's any of your business, but yes, of course I'd like to find someone who can love me, and who I can love—"

"As much as Sam," he interrupted.

"Yes. That much."

She shoved everything back in her pack and marched off to find a third trap site, not bothering to wait for him.

Over the past three years, every man she'd met had inevitably been compared to Sam—and fallen short. She always found something to fault in any man who threatened to engage her emotions. He was too tall. Or too short. Or too smart. Or not smart enough. His touch was too soft. Or too hard. It was like the three bears and their porridge. There was never a man who was "just right."

Have you forgotten how you felt in Luke Granger's arms?

That was an aberration.

Are you sure?

No, I'm not sure.

Don't you think you should check into the matter?

That could be dangerous.

Or perfectly wonderful.

All right. All right. I'll check it out. Maybe. If an opportunity presents itself. Which I doubt will happen.

Make it happen.

Luke followed closely on Abigail's heels and quickly caught up to her. "I don't believe in all this idealistic love stuff you're spouting," he said.

"That isn't surprising, considering your history," Abigail said. "But people *need* other people. I—"

"I don't *need* anyone," Luke contradicted. "I've managed fine by myself for the past ten years."

Abigail cocked a disbelieving brow. "Really?" She dropped to her knees at the third trap site. "What about your biological need for—" Abigail knew she shouldn't bring up the subject. But he was the one who'd started this conversation. She was going to finish it. "For sex," she finished.

For a moment Luke was speechless. He started to say he didn't *need* sex. The truth was, he'd been without a woman for longer than he wanted to admit. Long enough to know he needed one now. Long enough that he was finding it hard to be around Abigail Dayton without wanting her. So maybe she had a point.

"All right," he said. "Maybe I do need sex. But I don't have to love a woman to satisfy my sexual needs. And she doesn't have to love me to enjoy the act, either.'' *Put that in your pipe and smoke it, Agent Dayton.*

Abigail stopped what she was doing to stare at Luke in dismay. ''Oh, you're wrong,'' she said. ''So very wrong.''

''About which part am I wrong?'' he asked, sticking his hands into his back pockets to keep them from reaching out for her.

''About what a woman feels in a man's arms. There is always more than just sex involved,'' Abigail protested. ''A woman's feelings are never disconnected from…from the physical sensations that naturally occur when—''

Abigail found herself mesmerized by Luke's heavy-lidded gaze. When he knelt beside her, she had enough presence of mind to say, ''Stay on the ground cloth. I don't want to get any human scent near the trap.''

He obliged her, but there wasn't much room on the four-by-four-foot square of canvas, and when he had settled, no more than an inch separated their bodies. He reached across her to move a pine branch out of the way, and his forearm brushed against her thigh.

Abigail stiffened as the intimate contact sent a frisson of feeling through her frame. She ignored him, hoping he wouldn't notice her reaction to his touch.

A moment later he reached for another piece of debris, and their shoulders met. She held her breath until a small space once again separated them.

In a matter of minutes the sexual tension was unbearable. What made it worse was that Abigail couldn't ask Luke to stop without admitting that what he was doing was arousing her. But enough was enough.

"What, exactly, is it that you hoped to prove by this demonstration, Mr. Granger?" she demanded at last.

He glanced down at what was now plain evidence of how even these slight touches had affected him, then looked up and met her gaze. "That I don't have to love you to want you," he said.

Abigail quivered with unwanted desire.

"And you don't have to love me to want

me,'' he added, staring at the flush that had risen at her throat.

Abigail wasn't sure how to respond. To say she felt no physical response to him would be an outright lie. On the other hand, Luke might think her feelings weren't involved in her reaction to him, but she knew herself too well to believe otherwise.

However, she had no intention of letting this go any further. It was too dangerous a course of action even to consider. Abigail didn't let her thoughts ponder on why it was dangerous or exactly what was at risk. She only knew she couldn't let this…seduction… continue. Under the circumstances, there was only one thing to do.

''No,'' Abigail said.

Luke searched her face to discern her feelings. Her cheeks were flushed, but her features were carefully controlled, revealing nothing. ''No?''

Abigail swallowed hard and said, ''No.''

Luke hurt with wanting her. But she'd made her feelings crystal clear. ''Have it your way, Abby,'' he said in a voice harsh with controlled need. ''But don't lie to me—or to yourself—anymore. You're no different from any other woman. You can want a man without loving him—or even liking him very much.'' He stood abruptly and stalked over to lean back against the pine, not bothering to hide the evidence of his desire.

Abigail opened her mouth to try and explain that he was wrong, that her feelings were engaged, and snapped it shut again. If he knew the truth she would be vulnerable to him. She turned back to the task at hand and quickly finished setting the third trap.

"One more to go," Abigail said when she was done. "We can head back toward my pickup. The fourth trap goes near the dead sheep. The wolf may come back to feed on the carcasses.''

They didn't speak again until the last trap was set, and Abigail had dropped her pack in the back of the pickup.

"What's next?'' Luke asked.

"I need to talk with all the neighboring ranchers, to see if any of them have sighted the wolf or lost any stock.''

"Do you need me for that?''

Abigail wished to heaven she could say no. The truth was, it would be easier if she had someone local along. People were always more willing to talk to a familiar face than to a stranger. She settled for admitting, "It would help to have you along."

He swore under his breath. "Let's get some lunch at my place. Then, I'll take you around."

Abigail turned the truck around and headed back down into the Boulder River Valley. Somehow the drive back seemed much longer than the drive out.

Well, did you find out what you wanted to know?

Yes.

So what do you think?

I think I'm in serious trouble.

3

*Certain postures and gestures express the
inner state of the wolf; other wolves,
upon seeing this behavior, may respond in
characteristic ways, depending on their feelings.*

Luke spent the drive back down the mountain thinking. Maybe Abigail Dayton's mind had been saying no, but her body had been saying yes. So where did that leave him? He glanced at her from the corner of his eye. Her straight blond hair was blowing wildly around her face, which was set in serene lines. You would never have known to look at her that the woman was soft to the touch, or that she had a backbone like iron.

Damn it, he couldn't help admiring her. She was doing a man's job, and doing it well. Yet there was an obvious feminine side to her that hadn't been lost to her masculine pursuits. His brow furrowed. Still, he couldn't understand why he was attracted to her.

She came about shoulder-high on him—about the right height for her body to meet his in all the right places. But there wasn't even a handful of bosom on her, and she didn't have hips worth mentioning. It had to be those green, cat's eyes and that flawless skin that had captured his imagination. He wanted to see those eyes glazed with passion, and to know if her skin was as soft, smooth and peach-colored all over as it was on her face and neck.

He refused to consider the possibility that anything else about the woman—her character, her sense of humor, her sympathy and willingness to listen—had sparked his interest in her.

Miss Abigail Dayton would be around for at least a week. That was plenty of time to seduce her—and prove his point. Love wasn't necessary for a man and woman to have satisfying, not to mention downright enjoyable, sex. He had no doubt that by the time that renegade wolf had been caged, he'd have her in his arms and in his bed. It was a moment he was looking forward to with relish.

Shorty had lunch ready when they arrived. "Figured you two would work up a healthy appetite," he said, serving them each a hearty bowl of vegetable beef soup. He put a plate of grilled cheese sandwiches in the center of the table. "Help yourselves. There's apple cobbler on the counter cooling for dessert. I got some chores to tend to, so I'll just leave you two alone."

He winked broadly at Abigail and then at Luke before he headed back outside, letting the screen door slam behind him.

Abigail's narrow-eyed gaze dared Luke to say anything the least bit suggestive.

He opened his mouth and shut it once before he said, "Eat your soup. It's getting cold."

Abigail was more than happy to keep her mouth full eating, because then she didn't have to talk. She'd already found out more than she wanted to know about Luke

Granger. It was obvious the man had spent his entire life surrounded by the wrong kind of women. No wonder he was so cynical about her gender. She had half a mind to prove to him over the next week that he was wrong. But that would mean getting more involved with him than she wanted to be.

But there was no reason why she couldn't talk to him, try to change his mind. She didn't ponder too much on why it seemed so important to change his mind about women. But it was, so she might as well take advantage of the time she had with him to enlighten him on a few essential truths about the female sex.

Having come to this momentous decision, Abigail set down her spoon and said, "What attracted you most about the last woman you...uh...dated?"

Luke grinned, and she felt a flutter in the pit of her stomach. Considering what she knew, she couldn't possibly still be attracted to the man. She must just have eaten a mite too much of Shorty's soup.

"Are you sure you want to know that?" he answered.

Abigail nodded.

"Her looks."

"Well, there you have it," Abigail said with a great deal of satisfaction.

"Have what?"

"The reason why you've had so little success with women."

The grin disappeared. "I can have any woman I want," he countered.

"Oh. I didn't mean to suggest that you couldn't attract a woman," Abigail soothed. "Quite the contrary. I'm sure with your looks women fall all over themselves to get your attention."

Luke's eyes narrowed suspiciously. "What are you getting at?"

Abigail licked her lips nervously and said, "I only meant that you should spend a little more time getting to know a woman before you get more...uh...personally acquainted."

The grin was back, looking even more confident than before. "If that's an invitation, I accept."

Abigail's mouth fell open. "What?"

"That is what you're getting at, isn't it?

You're ready to admit that you want to go to bed with me, but you'd like us to get to know each other better first. Hell, lady, that's fine with me.''

Abigail's chair tumbled backward as she leapt to her feet. ''That most certainly is *not* what I was getting at!''

Luke found her immensely appealing, with her chin up and her green eyes flashing and her fisted hands perched on her slim hips. He set his spoon down and leaned forward with his elbows on the table, one strong hand laced through the other. ''I think the lady doth protest too much,'' he said in a quiet voice.

Abigail's face flushed scarlet.

Luke's brows lowered as a sudden thought struck him. He leaned back in his chair, put his laced hands behind his head and eyed her slowly from hip to hair. ''How long has it been, Abby, since you made love to a man? One year? Two?''

Abigail's eyelashes swept down, and her flush deepened.

''Aw, Abby,'' he said softly. ''It could be so good between us.''

Abigail opened her eyes and, for an instant, let him see her vulnerability.

"You look like a deer caught in a set of headlights."

Abigail wrapped her arms around herself, amazed at how well he'd read her fear of getting emotionally involved with a man... with him. A second later another set of arms surrounded her, strong arms, comforting arms, as she was pulled back into Luke's embrace.

"Don't be afraid, Abby," he murmured in her ear. "I won't let you get hurt. I—"

Abigail turned and put her hands against his chest to keep some space between them. "You don't understand." This wasn't what she wanted. Tenderness was too frightening. "Please don't do this, Luke."

Instead of letting her go, he tightened his hold. "Talk to me, Abby. Tell me what you're feeling."

"I feel foolish," she admitted with a tad more honesty than she'd intended. She stopped struggling. Luke was stronger than she was. She wasn't going to get away until he let her go.

She looked up at him, searching his face, not sure what she was hoping to find. She couldn't understand or explain her undeniable physical attraction to him. Yet, somehow, she had to find the words to make him keep his distance. "I've already told you that to me, making love is more than a means of satisfying sexual desire. So what do you want from me? Sam was a very special man. Living with Sam, loving him, was so wonderful because we had a lifetime of good memories together. How can I ever find that with another man?"

"By sharing the rest of your life with another man," Luke answered. "By making new memories to carry with you."

Startled by what he'd suggested, Abigail met Luke's smoky-eyed gaze. "That presupposes I can find another man I could love as much as Sam." Her eyes searched his as she admitted in a sad voice, "I don't think that's possible."

Suddenly he freed her.

"I'm sure as hell not volunteering for the job."

Abigail was confused by his vehemence and had no idea how to respond to it.

Luke never gave her the chance. "The only kind of memories I'm interested in creating with you are the kind that involve hot and heavy sex," he said. "You touching me, and me touching you, in ways that make us writhe with ecstasy in each other's arms. I'm talking about me being so deep inside you, filling you so full, that there isn't room for memories of another man's touch."

Luke had meant to frighten Abigail away, and he saw from the way she shrank from him that his tone of voice, and the ruthlessness of his words, had done their job. For a moment there, things had gotten a little scary. *Making memories.* That was the kind of fairy-tale hope that had gotten him married once upon a time. He wasn't about to travel down that trail again. There were too many pitfalls to lay a man low.

Abigail was watching Luke, so she saw the moment his gray eyes turned soft and yearning. He wasn't the callous bastard he wanted her to think he was. But as suddenly as it had appeared, the softness was gone from his eyes, and they were a bleak, flinty gray again.

"Well, Abby, you've heard my offer. What do you say?"

For a moment Abigail was tempted to say yes, just to call his bluff. But that wasn't honest, and more than anything, she wanted to be honest with Luke Granger. It seemed too few women had been.

"I have to say no, Luke," she answered in a low voice. "But if you're willing, maybe we can make a different kind of memories in the next week that I can take along with me when I go back to Helena."

Luke frowned. "What did you have in mind?"

"I'd like to be your friend. And I'd like you to be mine."

Luke made a dismissive sound in his throat. "I don't have any women friends."

"Maybe it's time you did."

"We don't have a damn thing in common to talk about," he said.

"I'm not so sure about that," Abigail replied with a twinkle of mischief in her eye.

"We could always debate the merits of cattle over sheep ranching in Montana."

"There isn't much you could say to convince me raising cattle makes as much sense as raising sheep," Luke said.

Abigail smiled. "We can discuss it between visits to the other sheep ranchers in the area. Shall we go?"

Without realizing quite how it had happened, Luke found himself ensconced in a deep conversation—some might have called it an argument—with Abigail over the advantages of raising a two-crop animal like sheep, versus raising cattle.

Sheep provided income both from wool in the spring and from lambs for slaughter in the fall. Meanwhile, cattle were raised for beef, the price of which fluctuated so much a rancher could be in clover one year and deep in Dutch the next.

Before he knew it, they'd arrived at Cyrus Alistair's ranch. Cyrus had died several months before and left a plot of land and about five hundred sheep to a grand-niece of his from back east. Luke tried to remember her name, but it wouldn't come.

What he could remember was how mad his best friend, Nathan Hazard, had been when Cyrus refused to let him buy the land, even when the ornery old cuss knew he was dying. This piece of property sat square in the middle of Nathan's sheep ranch, and Cyrus had been a thorn in Nathan's side for the fifteen years since the young man had come home from college and taken over the running of the ranch from his invalid father—who had been Cyrus's sworn enemy.

From what Luke had heard, the young woman who'd inherited the land from Cyrus was a greenhorn through and through. She'd been making mistakes—big mistakes—running the place that would soon have her so far in hock to the bank that she'd be more than willing to sell out to Nathan just to keep from losing her shirt.

"Oh, my God," Abigail said at her first sight of the ranch. If she'd had any doubts about how well-run Luke's sheep ranch was, she only had to take one look at the place at which they'd just arrived.

The small wooden pens, called jugs, for holding the new lambs and their mothers were broken down. A stack of dead lambs had been piled beside the barn. There were numerous mudholes on the road leading to the house that should have dried out by now—if there had been any drainage ditches dug. Fields that should have been planted with winter feed were lying fallow. This place was a disaster in the making.

Abigail angrily eyed the stack of dead lambs. How could anyone expect a wolf— or any predator for that matter—to ignore that kind of invitation? When she met this rancher, whoever it was, she was going to give him a good piece of her mind. "What did you say this rancher's name is? I can't believe he let his place get run down like this."

"I didn't. And *he* is a *she*."

Startled, Abigail turned to Luke and said, "I suppose you're going to say the reason the place looks like this is because a woman's trying to manage it. I can't believe that's all there is to it. Something must be wrong."

Luke cleared his throat. "Well, actually the problem is she's a greenhorn. Doesn't know the first thing about what she's doing.''

"I'm sure that as a good neighbor you offered her what help you could," Abigail said.

Luke shifted uneasily in his seat. "Well, you see, my friend Nathan, he—''

"I don't want to hear your excuses," Abigail said, cutting him off. She shoved the pickup door open and stepped down into a mud puddle. "Let's get this over with."

The moment Abigail saw the young woman, her heart went out to her. She was dumping slops into the pigpen, wearing bibbed overalls, a plaid wool shirt, galoshes on her feet, and a Harley's Feed Store baseball cap on her brown hair, which hung in two thick braids over her shoulders. She had an open, freckled face, but it was pale and drawn-looking. She was so tall, nearly six feet, and looked so physically strong that Abigail wondered why she hadn't made a better go of it.

"Hello," Abigail said, extending her hand. "Abigail Dayton, Fish and Wildlife."

A hesitant smile greeted Abigail's outstretched hand. The woman pulled a filthy glove off her hand, and an almost equally grimy and newly callused hand grasped Abigail's fingers. Abigail found herself wondering what she could do to help this woman succeed, where she was so obviously failing.

"My name's Harriet Alistair," the woman said in a surprisingly husky voice. She climbed over the top of the pigpen, instead of going through the gate, which was broken and had been wired shut. "People mostly call me Harry," the woman said as she joined them.

Harry. What a perfectly awful name for a woman, Abigail thought. There was nothing the least bit feminine about it. Although, to be honest, Harry couldn't be called your typical female. She defied description, not to mention the traditional role of a woman in the West, which was to stand by—or behind—her man.

When Harry looked inquiringly at Luke, he held out his hand and said, "I'm Luke Granger. Your neighbor to the south. Sorry

I haven't been over to see you sooner but…I've been busy.''

The excuse sounded lame to Luke's ears, and worse, he knew it wasn't the truth. He could have made time if he'd wanted to. Nathan had asked him to stay away, and in deference to his friend, he had. But he was starting to wonder how Nathan could leave this poor woman to fend for herself. Luke could see that despite her size and apparent strength she was exhausted.

Abigail saw the same thing as they all walked toward the small log cabin that served as a ranch house. ''I've come to ask if you've seen any wolves around here.''

Harry stopped dead in her tracks, and her brown eyes rounded as big as saucers. ''Wolves?''

Abigail saw that she'd frightened the woman and hurried to reassure her. ''They aren't any danger to you,'' she explained. ''As a matter of fact, there hasn't been a single recorded incident of a wild wolf seriously injuring or killing anybody in North America.''

''Ever?''

"Ever," Abigail confirmed.

Harry's brow furrowed in disbelief. "But wolves are so—ferocious!"

Abigail laughed as she followed Harry toward the back door of the dilapidated, and rather primitive, log ranch house, with Luke trailing behind them, a forgotten man.

"You're probably remembering all those fairy tales you heard as a child. 'The Three Little Pigs and the *Big Bad Wolf,*' 'Little Red Riding Hood and the *Big Bad Wolf,*' 'Peter and the *Big Bad*'—well, you get the idea. It just isn't so. The wolf is about the shyest creature around. That's why, aside from the fact that there aren't too many left anymore, you don't often see them."

Abigail controlled a gasp when they stepped into the kitchen. Total chaos. About a half-dozen bum lambs slept on wadded blankets in the corner of the unfinished wooden floor. The sink was piled high with dishes. The painted yellow cupboards hung open and appeared nearly bare of food. The counters were covered with cans of formula and nippled Coke bottles used to feed the lambs. It was easy to see why the tall woman looked so exhausted.

Harry stared at the mess without seeming to know what to do next, and Abigail felt angry for what the woman must be feeling right now, and frustrated by her inability to do anything to really help.

"I'd love some coffee," Abigail said. "Wouldn't you, Luke?"

Luke was also appalled. He'd had no idea the woman was in such distress. He remembered how Nathan had said he planned to "hang that damned tenderfoot out to dry." Luke felt guilty. In a voice meant to be encouraging to his new neighbor, he said, "Sure, uh…Harry, I'd love some coffee." It felt strange calling a woman by a man's name.

Having some direction, Harry set to with a will. While she was working, Luke and Abigail settled themselves at a chrome kitchen table strewn with numerous brochures. The depth of Harry's ignorance was apparent from the titles: *Sheep Raising for Beginners, Harvesting, Preparing and Selling Montana Wool* and *Wintering Montana*

Ewes. It was also apparent she was trying to learn the economics of the business from such titles as: *Making Your Farm Flock Pay* and *Managing Winter Sheep Range for Greater Profit.*

Harry Alistair wasn't a total fool if she recognized her own ignorance. But from the look of things, Abigail was pretty sure Harry was going to go bust long before she learned how to turn a profit managing sheep.

"I still find it hard to believe that wolves are as harmless to humans as you're suggesting," Harry said as she set down mugs of hot coffee in front of them. "If so, how did all those fairy tales ever get started? They must have had some basis in fact."

Abigail shrugged. "I suppose they might have started because wolves usually run in packs of ten to fifteen. That's an intimidating number of teeth to run into on a dark night. And they're ferocious hunters—of ungulates."

"Ungulates?" Harry said, slipping into a chrome-legged chair with a torn red plastic seat.

"Hooved animals—deer, elk and moose. Fairy tales have done the wolf a great disservice. I've learned over the years that wolves aren't the monsters of fairy tale legend. They're simply another predator that has to kill to survive."

Harry's smile reappeared, and the slight gap between her two front teeth gave her a winsome look. "What you're saying is a real relief. I've been meaning to learn how to shoot a gun in case I had trouble with predators, but—"

Abigail rose out of her chair like an avenging angel. "You can't *shoot* a gray wolf! They're endangered, and they're protected."

"I'm sorry," Harry said, her face a picture of despair. "I didn't know. There's so much I don't know!"

Abigail couldn't help responding to the other woman's wretchedness. She reached out a hand to comfort Harry, who'd hidden her face in her hands to conceal what, Abigail supposed from the hiccoughing sounds, had to be tears.

"I'm the one who's sorry," Abigail said.

"Whenever I start talking about wolves, I tend to get on my high horse."

Abigail peeked at Luke to see if he'd heard that admission, and sure enough he was eyeing her ruefully. "Anyway, all I wanted to find out today was whether you'd seen any wolves, and I take it that you haven't."

Harry dropped her hands to her lap and stared at them as she answered, "No, I haven't. And I don't care if I ever do."

"You shouldn't leave those dead lambs lying around, then," Abigail warned. "Or you're liable to see a wolf sooner than you'd like."

Harry lifted her face to reveal misery etched in the furrows of her brow. "I...I don't know what to do with the lambs," she admitted.

Luke's lips thinned into a severe line. Nathan or no Nathan, he wasn't going to let this woman go unassisted. "I'll take care of burying them," he said.

"But I can't afford to pay—"

"Neighbors don't have to pay one another for lending a helping hand," Luke said.

"If you two will excuse me, I'll see to those lambs right now."

"Is he always like that?" Harry asked when Luke was gone. "So helpful, I mean?"

"I don't know," Abigail answered. "I only met him this morning."

While Luke worked outside, Abigail had a chance to find out how and why Harry Alistair had decided to try to make a go of her great-uncle's sheep ranch. Once Abigail had heard the story, she had a great deal of respect for what Harry was trying to do. And a great deal of trepidation that she was doomed to fail.

The whole time Harry was talking, Abigail stayed busy, washing the dishes in the sink, gathering up the brochures on the table and closing cupboard doors. Slowly, but surely, the kitchen took on some semblance of order.

"Maybe you should accept this Nathan Hazard fellow's offer to buy you out," Abigail said.

"Never!" Harry retorted. "I'll let the place go to rack and ruin first. That man is

the meanest, ugliest son-of-a-bitch who
ever—''

Harry stopped in the middle of her tirade
as Luke Granger opened the kitchen door
and stepped inside. ''All finished. We have
time to visit another ranch or two before
supper if you're up to it,'' he said to Abigail.

Abigail turned and grasped Harry's hands.
''I wish you luck, Harry.'' She knew the tenderfoot rancher was going to need it.

Luke turned to Harry and said, ''If you're
ever in trouble, you call me. I'll be glad to
do what I can.''

Harry's freckles disappeared as she
blushed. ''Thank you, Luke. I wouldn't want
to be indebted to you for more than I could
repay.''

Luke slanted a glance at Abigail and said
with a perfectly straight face, ''Just doing
my neighborly duty, Harry. Be seeing you.''

Once they were back in the pickup and on
their way, Abigail heaved a big sigh.

''What was that for?'' Luke asked.

''She isn't going to make it, is she?''

"I doubt it," Luke admitted.

"It was kind of you to offer help."

"It was the least I could do," Luke replied, uncomfortable with the knowledge that he could have done a lot more, a lot sooner. And doubly uncomfortable with the warm feelings he got inside from Abigail's compliment. "Looked to me like you did your own share of helping."

"I couldn't do much," she replied with a troubled look. "Just washed a few dishes and stacked a few brochures. It sounded to me like somebody named Nathan Hazard is doing his damnedest to see that Harry fails."

"She doesn't need much help in that direction," Luke said.

"How can you say such a thing?"

"Because, unfortunately, it's true. It's another case of survival of the fittest, Abby. If she can't make a go of it, she should leave the land for someone who can," Luke said bluntly. "That's the way it's always been. That's the way it always will be."

Abigail shoved her fingers through her hair agitatedly. "It seems so sad. Harry told me she's never succeeded at anything she's ever tried. She was so determined when she came here to finally turn her life around.'' Abigail sought Luke's gaze. ''Isn't there anything anybody can do to help her?''

Luke's lips pressed into a thin line. He didn't like the way that look in Abigail's eyes affected him. He'd only met the woman this morning, and already he found himself wanting to please her. As much as he wanted to refuse to help, he found, after another look at those tear-threatened green eyes, that he couldn't. ''I can have a talk with Nathan Hazard,'' he said.

''You know him?''

''Harry's 'son-of-a-bitch' is my best friend.'' Luke grimaced. ''He isn't as bad as she paints him. I'm sure if I talk to him, we can work something out.''

''I'd like to have a word or two with Harry's nemesis myself,'' she said, her eyes glinting with determination. ''Point me in the right direction.''

''That's his place down there by the river. Before you jump in with both feet, Abby, maybe I ought to warn you about Nathan Hazard.''

''What about him?''

''I think he's what you women fondly call a male chauvinist pig.''

Abigail's lips curved into an amused smile. ''And you're not?''

''Can't hold a candle to Nathan,'' Luke answered.

Abigail sent a calculating look in Luke's direction. ''There's definitely more to you than meets the eye.''

''What makes you so sure?''

Abigail shrugged. ''A woman just knows these things.'' She had spent barely a day with the man, and already she was certain there were depths to him that he didn't want a woman to plumb. The minute Luke thought she might be slipping past the barriers he'd erected to keep her at arm's length, he became brusque and remote.

But a heartless man didn't help out a woman like Harriet Alistair and ask nothing in return. Or offer to take on his friend on her behalf. Or agree to put his lambs at risk to save a renegade gray wolf.

Abigail already liked what she'd seen of

Luke Granger. She was determined to know the real man, the one beneath all the bitterness and disillusion caused by a lifetime of disappointment in his relationships with women.

She tried to convince herself that her interest arose from a desire to foster a budding friendship. But the pounding blood in her veins, and the shivers down her spine whenever the man came near her, left the purity of her motives in doubt. The situation was complicated because she felt obliged to be as open with Luke about herself as she wanted him to be with her. That entailed a certain gamble Abigail had to weigh carefully before she committed herself to getting more involved with the rancher.

When Sam had died, Abigail had sworn off taking risks. During the past three years, she hadn't let any man get close. She simply couldn't take the chance of losing any more of her heart.

But there was something about Luke Granger, some indefinable part of him that called out to some part of her. And despite

4

As the mating season approaches, all interactions among pack members become more intense and frequent, including friendly contacts as well as conflicts and rivalries.

Abigail stared in awe at the tall, gorgeous male creature standing before her on the steps of a log house that was as huge, pristine and presentable as Harry's was tiny, dirty and decrepit.

"Howdy, ma'am," the man greeted Abigail in a deep, friendly voice. "Name's Nathan Hazard. What can I do for you today?"

This was Harry Alistair's mean, *ugly* son-of-a-bitch? Nathan Hazard had sapphire blue eyes, thick, wavy blond hair that hung down over his blue work-shirt collar, powerful forearms that showed to advantage beyond his rolled-up sleeves, long legs encased in a

pair of butter soft jeans and the sharp-planed
face of a model in an upscale men's maga-
zine. Abigail was struck speechless by his
perfection. It was left to Luke to make the
introductions.

"I'd like you to meet Agent Abigail Dayton from Fish and Wildlife," Luke said to
his friend.

Nathan shook Abigail's hand, but when
she remained mute he turned to Luke and
said, "Last I heard you'd called Animal
Damage Control about that wolf. What's
going on?"

Luke flushed. "It's a long story. I—"

"Come on in and have a cup of coffee,
and you can tell me all about it."

Before Abigail could protest that they
had a lot of places to get to before the sun
went down, and she only wanted to ask
whether he'd seen any wolves, Nathan had
ushered the two of them inside the A-frame
house. He seated them on the corduroy
couch and chair that faced a central copper-
hooded fireplace, and relaxed into an ancient wooden rocker across from them.

On the interior walls, the pine logs of

which the house was constructed had been left as natural as they were on the outside but were a lighter color because they hadn't weathered. The spacious living room was decorated in pale earth tones accented with navy. A tan, navy and rust braided rug snugged up under the furniture on the polished oak hardwood floor. The living room had a cathedral ceiling, with large windows at each end and on both sides, so that no matter where you looked there was a breathtaking view: the sparkling Boulder River bounded by cottonwoods to the east, the Crazy Mountains to the north, the snow-capped Absarokas to the south, and to the east, pasture dotted with ewes and their twin lambs, which had been joined by a grazing herd of twenty or so wild mule deer.

"This is beautiful," Abigail said in an awed voice. She couldn't decide which view she liked best. She craned her neck to check out the window behind her.

Luke and Nathan exchanged a knowing look. More than one woman had gotten starry-eyed over Nathan Hazard's house.

But Nathan hadn't built the house to attract a woman; he was still a bachelor. From everything Luke knew about him, Nathan intended to stay that way. He had designed the house to please himself and built it because he liked beautiful things. Luke's friend had studied to be an architect before a farm accident fifteen years ago had left his father an invalid, and cut those dreams short.

"There you are, Katoya," Nathan said, as an old woman appeared with a tray containing three cups, a white ceramic pot and a sheep-shaped creamer and sugar bowl. "I was going to ask for some coffee for my guests, but I see you're a step ahead of me."

Abigail recognized the diminutive woman's features—her dark brown eyes, broad forehead, straight nose, high cheekbones and thin-lipped mouth—as those of a Blackfoot Indian. Abigail had come to know many Blackfeet on the reservation that bounded Glacier National Park. The old woman's skin was a deep bronze and unlined, despite her great age, which was evidenced by her braided gray hair and gnarled fingers.

"I'm pleased to meet you, Katoya," Abigail said in the Blackfoot tongue. The woman's name meant Sweet Pine. The sweet pine was a fragrant balsam, sometimes mixed with grease and used by the Blackfeet as a perfume. It was a very romantic name, Abigail thought, and she wondered what kind of woman Katoya had been in her youth to earn it.

The old woman smiled with her eyes, rather than her mouth, and returned Abigail's greeting in Blackfoot. Then she turned to Luke and asked in English, "Is this your woman?"

Luke saw the amused look on Nathan's face as he waited to hear whether his friend would lay claim to the Fish and Wildlife agent. Luke let his gaze rove Abby's deliciously enticing body. What was he supposed to say? Wanting wasn't the same as possessing. If Abigail Dayton got her way, they would part as *friends*.

When Luke remained silent, the old

woman shook her head and made another comment in the Blackfoot tongue.

Abigail turned beet red.

"What did she say?" Luke demanded when Katoya had left.

"Nothing," Abigail lied. *Only that Abigail's man was hungry—for more than food—and Abigail should feed him or he would find another who would.*

"I didn't know you knew how to speak Blackfoot," Luke said.

Confused by the rush of desire she'd felt at the Indian woman's words and needing desperately to put some emotional distance between herself and Luke Granger, Abigail arched a brow and said, "There are a lot of things you don't know about me."

"I'm ready and willing to learn. All you have to do is say the word," Luke said, focusing his gaze on Abigail.

Nathan grinned at the sight of the sparks flying between his two guests but resisted the urge to tease his friend. Instead, he interrupted Luke's visual seduction of the Fish and Wildlife agent by asking, "What caused your change of plans regarding the wolf?'' Although, considering what he'd just seen, the answer seemed obvious. He covered his mouth to keep the laughter from erupting.

Luke kept staring at Abigail, refusing to release her from his sensual spell.

Abigail tore her gaze away from Luke and focused it on Nathan's face—which seemed a little rigid. She felt as though she'd escaped a terrible threat. She ought to feel relieved, but she felt more like crying. It had been a mistake to let her feelings get out of control like this. After Sam's death she'd grieved so long and so hard that it had been necessary to stop feeling, in order to get over her loss. She didn't want to feel pain again. She didn't want to feel anything again.

Abigail's forehead creased in confusion as she tried to remember what Nathan had asked. Oh, yes, why was she here instead of someone from Animal Damage Control? To her consternation, she had to keep her hands clasped in her lap to keep them from shaking as she explained, ''I convinced Luke to give me a chance to capture and relocate the wolf he sighted. I'm checking now to see if any other ranchers in the valley have sighted wolves or had problems with wolf depredation."

"Nope and nope," Nathan said. "But I'll be on the lookout and give you a call. Where can I reach you?"

"I'll be staying—"

"She'll be staying at my place," Luke interrupted.

Abigail felt as though the ground had fallen out from under her. She couldn't spend the night at Luke's house. In her current state of emotional upheaval, being a bedroom away would be too close for comfort. "It's not necessary—"

"You haven't got much time to catch that renegade," Luke said. "You'll have even less if you have to spend it driving back and forth to Big Timber."

What he said made a lot of sense. Surely she had enough self-control to resist Luke's overtures. She didn't fool herself that he wouldn't make them. All she had to do was reassert her desire to pursue a *friendship* with him.

"I'll be glad to accept your invitation." Abigail's sense of humor suddenly reasserted itself, and she managed to grin as she added, "If you're up to it, maybe we can have a good game of checkers after supper." She turned back to Nathan and said, "If you see any wolves, you can leave a message for me at Luke's place."

Luke exchanged a look with Nathan that spoke volumes. Both men understood, even if Abigail didn't, that Luke had plans to enjoy more than a game of checkers with Abigail Dayton after supper.

"By the way," Abigail said to Nathan. "We stopped off at Harry Alistair's place before we came here. She seems to be having a bit of trouble making a go of it." That was the understatement of the year.

A frown appeared on Nathan's face, and for a moment he looked every bit as mean and ugly as Harry had accused him of being. "That woman has no business trying to manage that ranch."

"I agree that she certainly needs some help. I'm surprised her neighbors haven't volunteered to provide some of it,'' Abigail said pointedly.

"She's an Alistair," Nathan retorted, as though that explained everything.

"What does that have to do with anything?" Abigail asked.

"Hazards have always hated Alistairs."

Abigail was incredulous. "Are you telling me you won't lift a finger to help Harry Alistair because of a *feud?*"

"That says it in a nutshell."

Abigail had a tremendous urge to call Nathan Hazard an idiot. But calling Nathan names wasn't going to convince him to help Harry Alistair. To hide her agitation she rose from the couch and walked over to the closest artifact—a bronze of a buffalo on a marble pedestal—and admired it.

The whole room was dotted with items of equal beauty, bronze sculptures and oil and watercolor paintings by famous Western artists. How could a man with a home this beautiful, who appreciated art this exquisite, act like such a narrow-minded idiot?

When she had control of her temper, Abigail turned to Luke and said, "He's your friend. Do you think you could talk him into changing his mind?"

Luke grimaced. Part of the reason he and Nathan had become such fast friends and stayed that way was because both men adhered strictly to the unwritten Code of the West.

The Code was a set of rules that had evolved when men first began to drift West, away from secret pasts, and toward a bold new future in a land that could be as merciless as it was bountiful. It included laws such as *Never ask a man where he comes from,* and *Never draw a gun unless you mean to shoot.*

Part of that Code was *Never offer a man advice unless he asks for it.* Abigail was asking him to break that unwritten rule. Luke heaved a sigh.

Nathan heard the sigh and asked, "Something troubling you, Luke?"

That was all Luke needed to hear. Nathan had asked. He could broach the subject now without offense. Nathan had made Luke promise not to help Harry Alistair, and it was likely Nathan had made sure no one else in the valley would lend a helping hand, either. Luke wanted Nathan to back off from that stand and give the woman a chance.

He leaned forward and rested his forearms on his widespread knees. "I know you want to get rid of Harry Alistair, but I think you're going about it the wrong way," Luke said earnestly.

Nathan's jaw clenched before he said, "Oh? What's the right way?"

"Since you asked," Luke said, flashing a relieved grin, "I think you ought to help her make a go of the place and encourage the rest of her neighbors to do the same. Then—"

"Wait just a damn minute," Nathan said, slamming his coffee cup down onto the small antique table next to the rocker.

"No, you wait," Luke said in a steely voice that kept Nathan rooted in his chair. "When was the last time you saw Harry Alistair?"

"I saw her two months ago, the day she

took over that old man's place," Nathan admitted.

"I suggest you make another visit. Take a good, long look around and see if you don't feel a little ashamed at the shabby way you've acted toward your new neighbor."

"I don't owe any Alistair a thing," Nathan argued.

"I've known you for a long time, Nathan," Luke said in a quiet voice. "But the way you've treated Harry Alistair is enough to make me question whether you're the kind of man I want to keep calling my friend."

Nathan's jaw worked as he absorbed Luke's hard words. "You're walking a narrow ledge, saying a thing like that."

"I wouldn't say it if I didn't mean it."

Nathan's eyes narrowed, his huge hands fisted, and his body tensed as though held under rigid control. "I think you'd better leave now."

Luke rose slowly, never taking his flinty gray eyes off his friend. "Come on, Abby.

Let's get out of here. I think we've about worn out our welcome.''

They were almost to the door when Nathan's voice stopped them. "Luke?''

Luke paused.

"I'll go see her again,'' he said quietly. "I won't promise more than that.''

"That's all I'm asking,'' Luke replied. He ushered Abigail out the door and closed it firmly behind them.

Luke remained silent as Abigail drove them to the next ranch in her pickup. She made no attempt to start a conversation, because she was doing some thinking. How strange that Luke would risk a friendship of long standing for a woman he hardly knew. More proof he wasn't the heartless bastard he'd tried to convince her he was. She pursed her lips in contemplation. The question that came to mind was, why had he been so anxious to have her believe the worst of him?

"Penny for your thoughts?''

Abigail wasn't ready to confront Luke about his benevolent behavior—especially since she was certain he would only deny it. Instead she asked, "Do you think Nathan will go visit Harry Alistair?"

"He gave his word. He won't break it."

"Will he let the feud get in the way of helping her?"

Luke picked at a frayed cuff on his sleeve. "The Hazard-Alistair feud has been going on a long time. There's a lot of bad blood between them."

"Harry's from back east," Abigail protested. "She doesn't have anything to do with the feud."

"Nothing about a feud ever makes much sense. I do know Nathan Hazard. Once he sees Harry Alistair, he isn't going to be able to walk away from her without lending a helping hand, any more than I could."

Abigail glanced at Luke from the corner of her eye. She wondered if he realized what he'd just admitted. Here was strong evidence that Luke's professed attitude toward women was laced with a well-camouflaged streak of kindness and consideration. At any rate, Abigail hoped Luke was right about Nathan helping out. Because she wasn't going to forget the look of despair in Harry Alistair's brown eyes for a long, long time.

They stopped at two more ranches before dark, but no one had seen any wolves or suffered any wolf depredations. Abigail sighed with relief when Luke's wood-frame house came into sight, because the silence between them had gotten decidedly uncomfortable.

It wasn't the silence, exactly, that was the problem. Quite simply, Abigail had become aware of every move Luke made. She'd watched the denim stretch over his thighs as he set his ankle on his knee. She'd seen the corded muscle ripple in his arms when he took off his felt Stetson to run a hand through his thick black hair. She'd felt a growing tightness in her belly as his hair-dusted fingers scratched what she was certain was a washboard belly.

What made the whole experience so unnerving was that she hadn't felt the least physical interest in any other man since Sam had died—until this morning when she met Luke Granger. Right now her entire body was alive, quivering with awareness of the man who sat totally relaxed beside her. It was enough to make her scream. Which, of course, she would never do, being a sane, rational kind of person. All the same, she kept her teeth gritted to make sure no sound got out. Which was why the truck had been so quiet since they'd left the last ranch house.

Despite what Abigail might have thought, Lukee was as conscious of her as she was of him. He'd kept his eyes straight ahead, knowing that to look at her was to desire her. But he could still smell her and feel her heat. His whole body felt on fire. He was burning alive, and the woman wanted to be his *friend.* He had to bite his lower lip to keep from laughing aloud. Which was why it had gotten so damned quiet on the ride home.

Luke bolted from the truck the instant they arrived at his ranch, saying he had to check on some things in the sheep buildings before he came inside. Abigail took advantage of the opportunity to take several deep, calming breaths before she headed into the house.

Apparently Shorty had done some cleaning during the day, because when Abigail walked through the front door of Luke's house, the items she'd had to step over at dawn had been removed from the living room floor. In fact, the furniture glowed with a rich sheen that reflected the licking flames crackling in the fieldstone fireplace.

Abigail was enchanted by the coziness of the small room. Nathan's house had been beautiful, but Luke's home possessed a warmth and charm that she found much more appealing.

Abigail could have made the same comparison between the two men. She found them both attractive. But somehow Nathan's astonishing handsomeness didn't cause her pulse to race the way Luke's striking features did.

"There you are," Shorty said as he entered the living room. "You ready to eat?"

"Hungry as a wolf," Abigail said with a grin.

Abigail turned when she heard the front door open, and her eyes locked with Luke's.

Luke swore under his breath. It had been

foolish to think he could rid himself of the need for her simply by taking a brisk walk in the cold night air. His need wasn't going to go away until it was quenched. He pressed his lips flat. The sooner they ate, the sooner Shorty would retire to his room, and the sooner he could have what he wanted—needed—from Abigail Dayton.

"You got some supper on the fire?" he said to Shorty.

"Just been awaitin' for you two to get here," he replied.

The instant they entered the kitchen the three orphan lambs came running toward Luke, baaing a noisy greeting. Abigail smiled when he stooped to pet each one in turn.

"I just fed them greedy little bums," Shorty said. "So don't you worry none 'bout them. Just set yourselves down and eat 'fore everything gets cold."

"I've invited Abby to stay with us while she's hunting that renegade," Luke told Shorty once the three of them had sat down to eat the Mexican casserole Shorty had prepared.

"I sorta 'spected that might happen," Shorty said with a twinkle in his eye. "So I made up the bed in the spare bedroom upstairs and dusted around a little. You need anything, Miss Abigail, you just holler."

"Thanks, Shorty."

As far as Luke was concerned, it took an eternity for supper to get eaten. He would have stolen Abigail then, except she volunteered to help Shorty with the dishes, and that sly old coot welcomed the help, even though he could see Luke had his desire on a short leash. Then Abigail invited Shorty to join her for a cup of coffee and a game of checkers in front of the fireplace. Although Luke was gnashing his teeth by then, Shorty just shot him a smug look and said, "I'd enjoy that right much. Gets so lonesome round here sometimes, I get to talking to myself."

Shorty made a point of sitting across from Abigail on the leather couch, the game board on the coffee table between them. Luke was forced to sit in the chair across the room while they played three games.

He finally lost his patience when he saw Abigail's eyelids slip closed as she listened to the end of one of Shorty's yarns. "I think maybe Abby has heard enough tall tales for one night." *But she's not done playing by a long shot.*

Abigail yawned. "I suppose I'd better get to bed. We've got an early day tomorrow."

Luke shot a killing glance at Shorty, who quickly gathered up the coffee cups from the end tables and said, "I s'pose you two need to make plans for tomorrow. I'll drop these in the kitchen and go on to bed."

Despite the coffee she'd just drunk, Abigail could hardly keep her eyes open. She yawned again. "Lord, I can't believe how tired I am."

"It has been a long day," Luke agreed. But *tired* was the last thing he was feeling.

Abigail was mesmerized by the sight of Luke's body flexing as he stood and stretched like a wolf ready for the hunt. An instant later, that powerful body settled beside her on the couch. She looked into

Luke's gray eyes and found a purely feral
gleam.

The hairs prickled on her neck and
gooseflesh rose on her arms. A wolf was on
the prowl. And she was its prey.

Luke's hands lightly grasped her shoulders from behind, and he began to knead
her aching muscles with his thumbs. "You
must be sore from carrying that heavy pack
this morning."

"Uh…a little." Suddenly Abigail wasn't
the least bit tired.

Luke's hands moved up under Abigail's
hair to massage her neck and sent a shiver
down her spine.

"Caught a nerve?" he murmured in her
ear.

Abigail shivered again and tried to laugh
at her powerful reaction to Luke's touch.
Her breath caught in her throat when his
hands lifted her hair so he could kiss her
nape.

Abigail shot off the couch as though
she'd been bitten, leaving Luke with his
empty hands hanging in the air. "I think I'd
better go to bed now," she said.

Abigail started up the stairs without looking back but had only gotten halfway up when she realized she had no idea which bedroom was hers. She turned around and found Luke on the step below her.

"Abby, I—"

Abigail put a hand on his chest to keep him where he was. The feel of hard muscle under her fingertips set her pulse to pounding. "Don't come any closer."

"I want you, Abby."

She put the other hand against his lips. "And don't say anything."

He reached up ever so slowly and took the hand she held against his lips and turned it so he could kiss her palm, and then her wrist. "I want you."

Abigail's knees felt wobbly. He had to stop doing what he was doing or she wouldn't be responsible for the consequences. "Please don't say things like that."

"Why not?"

"I thought we were going to be friends."

"We are," he said with a smile.

"Friends don't—"

"Friends do."

Abigail moaned as Luke took one of her fingers into his mouth and sucked on it.

"I don't even know you," Abigail said, her whole body trembling as Luke bit the pad between her thumb and forefinger.

"You know everything you need to know about me."

"I doubt that," Abigail said breathlessly.

"Ask me anything."

"Do you have any social diseases?"

Luke's head jerked up in surprise. "Do I *what?*"

Well, that certainly broke the mood. "I mean," Abigail continued in a firm voice, "that a woman can't be too careful nowadays."

Luke smiled. "I don't have any social diseases," he said. "Anything else you'd like to know?"

"Uh...do you have any...uh...protection?"

"You're not protected?"

Abigail blushed and licked her lips. "No."

Luke swore under his breath and let her

go. He shoved his fingers through his hair in frustration, then gripped the banister with both hands. She had as much as admitted she hadn't had a man since her husband had died, so there would have been no need for her to be protected. Unfortunately it had been so long since he'd had a woman, he didn't have any protection handy, either. Luke swore again. "I don't have a damn thing in the house."

Abigail breathed a sigh of relief.

"You don't have to act so damned happy about it," Luke said.

Abigail put a hand lightly on his shoulder. "You'll thank me for this in the morning."

Luke stared at her in disbelief and then laughed out loud. "Only a woman could make an idiotic statement like that."

"I don't want to have sex with you, Luke." She paused and added, "And I don't love you, so making love is out of the question." She softened what she'd said with a friendly smile and finished, "Now that we have that settled, tell me, which bedroom is mine?"

There was a moment of poignant silence before he said, ''Last door on the left at the end of the hall.''

Abigail leaned forward and pressed her lips lightly against Luke's, savoring the softness of his mouth. ''Good night, Luke,'' she whispered.

Luke watched her hips sway as she walked up the stairs and imagined himself with his hands around her waist walking right behind her, her backside rubbing up against him. He groaned. His body was taking a real beating, and Abigail Dayton had barely laid a finger on him.

She'd also given him a lot of food for thought. She was the first woman in his memory who hadn't been willing to settle for sex. And he wasn't interested in more than that. Normally he would have kissed her good-bye and sent her on her way. Somehow that solution didn't even occur to him in relation to Abigail Dayton. It was entirely possible that he could seduce her; she was not indifferent to him. But knowing how she felt about sex…and making love…it was also clear that seducing her might cause her pain in ways he didn't want to contemplate. So where did that leave him?

With a lot of thinking to do.

"Abby?" he called up to her.

Her voice came down to him from the hallway upstairs. "Yes, Luke?"

"Can you ride a horse?"

"Yes. Will we be riding tomorrow?"

"Yes. Good night, Abby."

"Good night, Luke."

Luke hoped that renegade wolf didn't get himself caught in one of those traps Abby had laid today. Because he hadn't finished stalking Abigail Dayton. Before he was done, he would figure out a way to capture her—and make her his—without committing his soul to do it.

5

*Male wolves generally initiate three times the
number of courtship actions as females do.*

Abigail stared with dismay and disgust at
the trap she had so carefully set the previous day. "It's sprung! Just like all the
others. That sneaky, three-toed renegade
sprang my traps. And he didn't leave so
much as a hair behind to show which way
he went."

"I'd be willing to bet he lost that fourth
toe in a steel trap," Luke mused, "and
learned a hard lesson he hasn't forgotten."

"Damn his wily hide!"

Abigail stepped down off the bay horse
she was riding and strode over to pick up
her leg-hold trap—the last to be collected.
The first trap had been sprung with no other

sign of the renegade than a soft paw track in the dust. The second trap had likewise been sprung, but had contained a rabbit, which had been half eaten by the wolf. The jaws of the third trap had closed on a branch of juniper that had been dragged across it.

Abigail hadn't really held out much hope that the fourth trap, the one at the creek, would have caught the wolf, but she was still disappointed to discover that the cunning renegade had dispatched her efforts as easily here as at the other three sites.

"Has this ever happened before?" Luke asked.

"Not to me. Not like this. I mean, there have been traps sprung by the wrong kind of animal, or by a branch falling from a tree, but I've never seen the likes of this. That wolf *deliberately* sprang these traps."

"What now? Will you set the traps again?" Luke asked.

"What good would that do?" Abigail snapped. "He would just spring them again." Abigail knew she shouldn't take out her frustration on Luke. It wasn't his fault the wolf was so smart. She slung the fourth trap into one of the saddlebags on the pack mule Luke led, which held all her supplies and the rest of the traps she'd collected. She wouldn't be needing her tranquilizer gun, or the cage she'd hoped to use on the wolf once it had been captured. Abigail leaned her forehead against the canvas pack and took a deep breath. "I'm sorry. I'm not usually so short-tempered."

The truth was, she hadn't gotten much sleep last night. She was tired and therefore cranky. She wanted to blame Luke for that, too, but in all honesty, once she'd left him behind on the stairs, she hadn't heard a peep out of him the rest of the evening. Abigail had lain in bed staring at the ceiling in the dark, wondering what would have happened if she had let him carry her upstairs to his bedroom, which it had turned out was across the hall from hers. Her fantasies had been vivid and uncomfortably sensual.

Abigail had been relieved to see the pale gray light of dawn. She'd dressed quickly and joined Luke for breakfast. He'd suggested they trailer horses and a pack mule up to the edge of the forest, since they could make better time getting to the traps on horseback.

Abigail was grateful now that she'd agreed. It would have been infinitely more frustrating to tramp back down the mountain on foot and empty-handed. "I've got to get to a phone and call my office in Helena," she said.

Luke cocked an inquiring brow.

"I need to arrange to have a helicopter flown down here, so I can do an aerial survey. If I can find the wolf, I may be able to tranquilize him from the air."

"That would take some pretty fancy shooting," Luke said, standing in the stirrups to stretch his legs.

"I'm a pretty fancy shot," Abigail retorted, as she remounted. She was feeling singed by her failure to catch the wolf. She didn't need Luke throwing coals on the fire, questioning her ability.

"If this isn't a renegade," Abigail continued, "if it's actually half of a breeding pair, there might be pups. The den, if there is one, won't be far from water, so I'll start my search along the East Boulder River and follow up along the creeks.''

As they rode back down the mountain, Abigail forced herself to concentrate on the beauty of the day, the sunshine, the piney air and the gorgeous wildflowers. It didn't help. She felt agitated and distraught. Why was she so upset that the wolf had sprung her traps? Of course, there was the concern that she might run out of time to capture the renegade.

But that wasn't really the problem. The truth was, she'd wanted to prove to Luke that she was good at what she did, and she'd been embarrassed by the failure of her best efforts. And anyway, why was it so important to her what Luke Granger thought? Abigail had been assiduously avoiding that question all morning. Because the answer was—

''How did you learn to speak Blackfoot so well?''

Abigail welcomed Luke's interruption with the same relief as a rodeo bronc rider who sees the pickup man coming after the eight-second buzzer sounds. She cleared her throat and said, "I studied anthropology in college and wrote my senior thesis on the Blackfoot Indians. That's when I learned most of what I know. When Sam and I were assigned to Glacier National Park, I got back in touch with some of the Blackfeet I'd met while in college and had a chance to practice what I knew."

"Why become a park ranger when you have a background in anthropology? Why aren't you off somewhere studying Indian artifacts?"

Luke watched Abigail's eyes take on a wistful look as she said, "Actually, I was offered a graduate assistantship to work with a noted anthropologist studying the origin of the Blackfoot language. I had already decided to accept it when my parents were killed."

"So you married Sam Dayton instead of following your dreams."

Abigail frowned. "I never gave up my dreams."

"So why aren't you studying Indian dialects right now, instead of setting traps?" Luke asked.

Abigail drew in a sharp breath. "Because there's such a thing as being practical," she replied. "I have to earn a living."

"Sam didn't have life insurance?"

"It went to his parents."

"You said you grew up on a cattle ranch. Didn't your parents leave you anything?"

"My brother, Price, got the ranch. There wasn't much else."

"I didn't know you had a brother."

Abigail smiled ruefully. "I told you before, there's a lot you don't know about me."

"Surely your brother would have been willing to help out if you'd asked."

"Price and I never really got along," Abigail said.

"I'd have guessed that with such loving parents, you and your brother would be close."

"Price was ten years old when I was born. By the time he was twenty, he'd left home. We never had much to do with each other. By his choice, not mine," Abigail said.

"Yet he got the ranch. That hardly seems fair."

"Nobody said life is fair," Abigail returned. "Besides, Sam and I had other plans."

"You mean, Sam had plans, and you went along because you were married to him," Luke said with an insight that Abigail found frightening.

She heaved a frustrated sigh. "You just don't understand."

"I'd like to," Luke said in a soft voice. "Why don't you explain it to me?"

Abigail met Luke's gaze and found a wealth of warmth and comfort. They had reached a mountain meadow, so they could ride side by side. When Luke reached out a hand to her, it seemed the most natural thing in the world to clasp it.

"I suppose I didn't feel like I was giving up my dreams when I married Sam, because Sam had always been a part of those dreams. Abigail sighed. "Sometimes I wonder how my life might have been different if my parents hadn't died. I mean, I still believe I would have married Sam...

eventually. Things don't ever turn out the way you expect, do they?''

Luke didn't answer, but it wasn't a question that called for an answer. They rode in silence for several minutes before he said, "I suppose I was curious about your broken dreams, because I've watched a few dreams of my own bite the dust. I wondered how you handled the disappointment.''

"I try to look forward, instead of back," she said quietly. "I try to remember what Sam and I had together and forget everything else.''

Abigail watched Luke's lips thin into a bitter line and his eyes harden before he said, "Some things are hard to forget. Or to forgive.''

"Like what?''

"Like your wife telling you in one breath that she's pregnant…and in the next, that she got rid of your child.''

Abigail gasped and reined her horse to a stop. Her hand tightened on Luke's as their eyes met—his full of pain, hers full of compassion. The look in his eyes changed, the pain becoming a somber sadness as he accepted the comfort she offered. Then it changed again, to one of need. It felt as though a band constricted her chest, and she couldn't breathe. She started to pull her hand from Luke's, but he reached over and curled an arm around her waist, lifting her out of her saddle and onto his lap.

"Luke, I—"

He cut her off, his mouth seeking hers as though he were a man dying of thirst, and she was life-giving water. It was a kiss of resurrection, of rebirth, of new life. It was a kiss of hope.

Abigail met his touch with willing lips as her hands circled his neck and then slid up into his hair, knocking his hat from his head.

"Abby, Abby," Luke whispered between kisses. "I need you. I need your warmth. I need your touch."

Abruptly Luke stopped kissing her, as though he had suddenly realized what he'd said.

They were both breathing hard, and Abigail felt the sweet ache of desire in her belly and breasts. She was sitting across him in such a way that it was impossible not to know that Luke was also aroused. Yet he had stopped.

"What's wrong?" she asked softly.

Instead of speaking, he kissed her again. This kiss was different from the ones before. It still aroused, it still implored, but there was something missing. Abigail leaned back and searched Luke's face to try and discover what it was he'd given before, that he now withheld. He still wanted her. That much she could see. What was gone was the vulnerability, the *need*, that for a brief time had been naked in his eyes.

"Let me go," she said.

Luke felt the resistance in Abigail's body and searched out her expressive green eyes to see whether she meant what she'd said. Her eyes were troubled and showed no remnants of the desire that had been there only moments before. He let go of her and helped her slide off his horse onto the ground. Before she could remount, he slid his leg over the saddle and landed on the ground beside her. He casually reached down and retrieved his hat from the ground where it had fallen and replaced it on his head, pulling it down low, leaving his face shadowed.

"Would you care to tell me what just happened?" he said.

"I think I could ask the same question of you."

He rested his hands on her hips and brought her flush against him, so she could feel his need. "A moment ago you were willing," he murmured, nudging himself against the soft cradle of her thighs.

"I changed my mind."

"Maybe I can change it again," he said with a coaxing grin.

"Look, Luke," Abigail said in her most reasonable voice. "This isn't a good idea."

His mouth found the soft skin at her throat and nibbled there. "I think it's a very good idea."

"I have work to do," Abigail insisted, valiantly attempting to ignore what he was doing. "A wolf to catch before he eats any more of your sheep."

"He can help himself to dinner on me,"

Luke said as his lips trailed up the slender length of her neck.

"You don't really mean that," Abigail said in a breathless voice. "Be sensible, Luke."

He caught the lobe of her ear in his teeth and bit it gently.

The blood raced in Abigail's veins. Luke was making it devilishly hard to concentrate on what was important: her job. That was where she had found solace after Sam's death. That was where she would find solace when Luke was gone from her life. She was proud of what she did and how well she did it.

Luke's tongue dipped into her ear.

Abigail moaned deep in her throat, a keening sound of need.

"The grass is soft here," Luke crooned in a husky voice. "We'll have the sun on our skin, the wind caressing our naked bodies. When was the last time you made love with nothing more than the big blue sky above you, Abby?"

When Abigail jerked away with a wounded cry, Luke knew he'd hit a nerve.

He took one look at her pale face and said with certainty, "You were with Sam."

When Abigail shuddered, Luke knew he was right. He also knew when he'd run into a wall he couldn't go around, a wall he couldn't go over. Sam Dayton, the wonderful. Sam Dayton, the heroic. He had about had his fill of Sam Dayton, the damned perfect ghost!

"You've got a phone call to make, and I've got business that needs tending. We'd better get going," he said as though it were she, and not he, who'd caused their delay getting down the mountain.

Before Abigail could voice a word to stop him, Luke put his hands on either side of her waist and lifted her back into the saddle. He remounted his chestnut in a smooth vault and kneed the gelding into a fast walk, tugging the pack horse along behind him.

Abigail followed Luke back to where they'd left the horse trailer without another word being spoken between them. She felt like hissing and spitting and clawing. It wasn't her fault Luke kept making passes at her that she didn't welcome.

You didn't enjoy his kisses?

I didn't want him to kiss me.

You didn't answer the question. Did you enjoy his kisses?

Yes.

So what stopped you?

Sam. Memories of Sam.

Maybe it's time to follow your own advice. Look forward, not back.

Abigail sighed so loudly that Luke stopped to stare at her before he shot home the bolt on the horse trailer, locking the three animals inside.

"I'm not going to ask what that was all about," he said. "Just get in the pickup, and let's get out of here."

The silent ride home gave Luke too much time to think. He'd surprised himself back there on the meadow. Where was the Luke Granger who had sworn he was never going to let another woman get under his skin? Hell, a few more minutes and they would both have been lying in the sweet, tall grass, bare-assed naked. And he still didn't have a damned bit of protection with him. He must be out of his mind. Crazy. Crazy with want. Crazy with *need*.

That thought brought him up short. Luke Granger didn't *need* a woman. He'd managed fine without the kind of pain and heartbreak *needing* a woman caused a man. He wasn't about to let this honey-blond, green-eyed seductress lure him into a trap he couldn't escape.

The instant they arrived at Luke's house, Abigail excused herself and headed inside to use the phone in the kitchen.

After Luke had unloaded the animals, he came in through the kitchen door to find Shorty putting away groceries. Abigail stood with her back to him, talking in a low voice on the phone.

"I got them 'necessary' supplies you wanted from the drugstore," Shorty said.

Luke's eyes widened in alarm when he saw what Shorty held in his hand. He gestured wildly for Shorty to hand the item to him.

Shorty held out the box of condoms and looked at it. "You didn't say how many to get," he said. "So I got a couple dozen.

Hope that's enough." The twinkle in Shorty's eyes was evidence of his teasing.

During the course of her conversation on the phone, Abigail turned to face Luke, who flushed a dull red, praying that Shorty wouldn't hand the condoms to him while Abigail was watching. There was nothing to be ashamed about in caring enough to take precautions. It reminded him that when he'd been on the mountain with her, the thought of protection, of making sure she didn't get pregnant with his child, had been the last thing on his mind. He wasn't ready to consider what that might mean.

Only now Luke wished he hadn't involved Shorty by asking him to pick up the condoms for him. He could take whatever ribbing the old man gave him, but he didn't want Abigail embarrassed by the situation. He realized now that what had been all right with other women, wasn't all right where Abby was concerned. He wished he'd kept his intentions toward her more private. But Luke had no idea how to cut off Shorty's teasing without apprising Abigail of the problem. He gritted his teeth and prayed.

"I didn't realize these come in so many varieties," Shorty said. "I got an extra box, to make sure I got the right kind."

Shorty pulled another equally large box of condoms out of the paper bag. He held one box in each hand and grinned. "Here you go."

Luke scowled.

Abigail, thinking the look was for her, abruptly turned her back on him.

Luke took quick advantage of the moment, stuffing the two boxes of condoms back into the paper bag from which Shorty had withdrawn them. He chastised Shorty with a sharp look before he grabbed the bag and headed out of the kitchen. "I'll go put these away."

"You just do that," Shorty said with a chortle of glee. "Someplace where they won't be too hard to reach when the time is right."

Luke brushed against Abigail on his way out of the room, and both of them tensed. Luke clutched the bag to his chest and mumbled, "Medicinal supplies. Go in the bathroom upstairs. Always put them away myself to save Shorty the trip.''

Abigail's brows rose in confusion.

Shorty guffawed.

Luke glowered ferociously at Shorty before stomping off up the stairs.

When Abigail finished her call she turned to Shorty and asked, ''What was that all about?''

'''Spect you'll find out soon enough,'' he said with a secretive grin. ''You gonna get that helicopter you want?''

''Not this afternoon,'' Abigail said. ''Our regular pilot is ferrying somebody else around in another part of the state. He'll be here first thing in the morning.''

''You got any plans for the rest of the day?'' Shorty asked.

Abigail leaned back against the wall. ''I have plans for the evening, but nothing this afternoon.''

''What plans?'' a voice beside her said.

Abigail turned to find Luke standing in the kitchen doorway. ''I thought I'd take a drive tonight and see if I can howl up any wolf pups.''

Luke breathed an inner sigh of relief. For a moment there he'd thought maybe she was going to meet someone—a man—in town. The ridiculousness of that possibility hit him a moment later, and he felt chagrined at the jealousy that had provoked such a thought. But she wasn't going anywhere tonight without him.

Luke had heard of howling up wolves, although he'd never tried to do it himself. It involved driving around dark forest roads and stopping at intervals to howl like a wolf. The human wolf howls, even though they weren't authentic, would be enough to set wolf pups to answering. It was the same principle as a town dog howling when it heard a siren. By locating the pups, Abigail would be able to pinpoint the den, and thus, the adult wolf or wolves. Assuming such a den with pups existed.

"If you don't have other plans, maybe you'd like to go with me this afternoon," Luke said.

"Go where?"

"Over to Harry Alistair's place." Luke grinned. "I got a call from Nathan early this morning asking if I could spare some time to help do repairs. I told him I'd get over there today if I could.''

Abigail met his grin with one of her own. ''I'm sure I could find something to keep me busy, too.''

They ate a quick lunch before driving over to the Alistair ranch. The scene that greeted them wasn't exactly what they'd been expecting.

Nathan was bent over a tractor engine near the barn, his shirt off and a fine sheen of sweat glistening on his broad shoulders. Harry was standing next to him, her fists on her hips, her face set in severe lines.

Abigail and Luke exchanged guilty glances. They were both responsible for Nathan being there. It didn't look like Harry was too happy about the situation.

''Hello, there,'' Luke said as he and Abigail approached the other couple.

''Hello,'' Harry muttered through clenched teeth. Her angry eyes remained on Nathan.

Nathan kept his head down and his hands busy. ''I ran into a little problem,'' he said.

"The tractor needs some work before I can do anything about that fallow field."

"Anything I can help with?" Luke asked Nathan.

Harry whirled on him, and Luke was stunned by the fierce light in her brown eyes. "You can turn that truck around and drive right back out of here."

"We came to help," Abigail said.

"I don't need your charity," Harry said in an anguished voice. "I don't need—"

Nathan suddenly dropped his wrench on the engine with a clatter and grabbed Harry by the arm, forcing her to face him. "That'll be enough of that!"

"Just who do you think you are?" Harry snarled. "I didn't ask you to come here. I didn't ask you to—"

"I'm doing what a good neighbor should do," Nathan replied.

"Right! Where was all this neighborliness when I had lambs dying because I didn't know how to deliver them? Where was all this friendly help when I really needed it?"

"You need it right now," Nathan bellowed, his grip tightening. "And I intend to give it to you."

"Over my dead body!" Harry shouted back.

"Be reasonable," Nathan said. "You need help."

"I don't need it from you," Harry replied stubbornly.

"Maybe you'd let us help," Abigail said, stepping forward to place a comforting hand on Harry's other arm, wanting to separate the two combatants and not sure how to accomplish it.

Harry's shoulders suddenly slumped, all the fight going out of her. She bit her quivering lower lip and closed her eyes to hold back the threatening tears. Then her shoulders came up again, and when her eyes opened, they focused on Nathan Hazard, flashing with defiance. "I want you off my property, Nathan Hazard. Now. I…" Her voice caught in an angry sob, but her jaw stiffened and she finished, "I have things to do inside. I expect you can see yourself off my land." Harry turned and marched toward the tiny log house without a single look back to see if he had obeyed her command.

Abigail shot a condemnatory look at Nathan. "I think I'll go see if there's anything I can do in the house to *help*." She pivoted and headed for the log house after Harry.

"What the hell happened here?" Luke demanded of his friend. "I asked you to come see the woman to help her out, not to make her mad...or cause her pain."

Nathan turned away from Luke and bent over the tractor engine searching for the lost wrench, which he quickly found. "She doesn't want my help," he said, tightening a bolt that was already as tight as it was ever going to be.

"There's such a thing as tact," Luke said dryly. "You don't have to force help down her throat."

"I don't think she'll take it any other way," Nathan said, his eyes bleak. He turned and leaned a hip against the tractor, wiping his greasy hands on what had once been a clean blue chambray shirt. "I don't understand that woman at all," he complained to Luke. "All I did was tell her a few things she was doing wrong and—"

"You did what?"

"I just told her..." Nathan stopped scrubbing at his hand with the shirt. "I shouldn't have been so blunt, I suppose..."

"You suppose?" Luke said incredulously.

"Aw, hellfire, Luke. I don't know a damn thing about talking to a woman. Just enough to say please and thank you and hand me my hat, I'll be going now. How was I supposed to know I'd hurt her feelings?"

"I'll agree there's no understanding a woman," Luke said, rubbing the back of his neck, "but surely you could do a better job of hanging on to your temper."

"I don't know about that," Nathan admitted in a raw voice. "Every time I get around that woman my self-control flies out the window. I can't even talk to her without getting into an argument. She's so damned stubborn—"

"And I suppose you're not," Luke interrupted.

"But I'm right, and she's wrong," Nathan protested righteously.

Luke burst out laughing and leaned against the tractor beside his friend. His laughter suddenly died in his throat. He rubbed his eyes with the heels of his hands. "Oh, my friend, I know exactly how you feel."

Nathan raised a speculative brow. "Abigail Dayton?"

He nodded.

"What do I do now?" Nathan asked, truly bewildered.

"Hell if I know," Luke said, shaking his head. He looked toward the house where Abigail had disappeared with Harry. "Maybe you'd better go back to square one and start over."

"I wish I'd never met Harry Alistair," Nathan said vehemently.

Luke opened his mouth to say the same thing about Abigail Dayton and snapped it shut again without speaking. He turned his back on Nathan and stared out over the fallow field they had come here to plow. His life in the past ten years had been a lot like that field.

Then Abby had come along, determined to make him see that love could grow where it had lain dormant for far too long. Luke could feel the slash of new furrows in his heart. Abby had planted seeds there. Luke wasn't sure whether he wanted to nurture them, or let them die. He only knew things weren't the same anymore. Not since Abigail Dayton had come into his life.

"Give it another try," Luke advised Nathan. "Maybe you'll have better luck next time." It was advice that could apply equally well to his own situation. If only he weren't too set in his ways, too damned stubborn, to take it. After all, what did he have to lose?

His heart.

In the past, when things had gone wrong, he'd picked up the broken pieces of his heart and slowly, carefully, put them back together again. What he had left was a fragile organ that couldn't take another break without shattering once and for all. Luke couldn't take the chance. He couldn't endure that kind of pain again. The past had taught him hard lessons, and he'd learned them well. He wasn't about to give any woman, not even Abigail Dayton, the chance to make a suffering fool out of him again.

6

Once a wolf begins howling, other pack members show a strong tendency to approach that animal and join the chorus.

Abigail turned her face to the night sky, took a deep breath, and let out a long, loud, ululating sound.

"Aaaaaoooooohhh."

She paused, waiting for a response, then howled again.

"Aaaaoohhhooohhhooohh."

Luke felt a chill down his spine. She did a pretty good imitation of a wolf. "Don't you feel a little silly doing that?"

Abigail grinned, her teeth showing white in the moonlight. It was the fourth or fifth stop they'd made, so she'd already done quite a bit of howling. "It's kind of fun, actually," she said. "You ought to try it."

"I'd feel ridiculous."

"I promise not to laugh."

Luke thought about it for a moment. "If you tell a single soul I did this, I'll deny it."

"Your secret is safe with me." Abigail crossed her heart with her finger. "Cross my heart and hope to die."

Luke stared at her warily for another moment, then turned to stare off into the darkness of the forest. They were standing next to Abigail's truck on the side of a dirt road in the mountains. He looked both ways for headlights or lights from a ranch house that would indicate anyone else might be close enough to hear him if he decided to indulge in this foolishness. He had to be insane to even think about howling at the moon.

He took a deep breath, turned his face to the sky, and produced a low, throaty sound.

"Aaaaaoooooooo."

Abigail bit her lips to keep from laughing. He sounded more like a wounded bear than a wolf. "Try again," she urged. "Think of every wolf howl you ever heard on the Late-Late Show. Then relax, and let the sound come out.''

"I feel stupid."

"You're doing fine."

Luke shifted his stance uneasily. He felt like a kid again, not a thirty-five-year-old man. He found himself grinning. So, who said an old man like himself couldn't have fun like a kid?

He shook his hands as though he were getting ready for some bulldogging, took several deep breaths, as though he were about to leave the chute on a wild bronc, and cleared his throat as though in preparation for some serious cowboy crooning. Then he turned his face upward until it was bathed in moonlight, opened his mouth and let the sound issue forth.

"Aaaaoohhohhoooohhhh."

Abigail's mouth dropped open in amazement. She held her breath, waiting for the sound to die. "That was wonderful! You sounded just like a wolf. Do it again."

Luke grinned boyishly. "I think I'll stop while I'm ahead."

Abigail laughed. "All right. I'm ready to call it a night, anyway. If there had been any pups around here, they'd have joined us by now. I guess we'd better head back."

"I'm sorry this didn't work," Luke said as he and Abigail turned toward her pickup.

Abigail shrugged. "It was worth a try to howl up some pups. But it looks like you're probably right, and we're looking for a lone wolf. At least you haven't lost any more sheep today."

"Maybe the wolf has moved on. Headed north or south out of the area," Luke said.

"That's always a possibility," Abigail conceded. "It's just as likely this renegade has established a territory around here. I'll have to keep looking until I know for sure."

"Or until your ten days are up," Luke said in quiet voice.

Abigail stopped in her tracks and turned to face him. "I'm grateful for what you're doing, Luke. Not many ranchers would be willing to risk losing stock to save a gray wolf."

He stuck his hand in his back pockets.

"My motives aren't quite as generous as you're making them sound."

"Oh?"

"I have to admit the thought of spending time in your company influenced my decision."

"Oh."

"I haven't made any secret of my attraction to you, Abby."

"I'm only here to do a job—"

"And doing it very well. But you know what they say, all work and no play… How would you like to go for a swim?"

"A swim?" Abigail laughed. "It's got to be around fifty degrees tonight."

"More like forty-five. But I know a great place to swim that's not too far off. We could be there in under an hour. What do you say?"

"I don't have a suit."

"You don't need one."

"I beg your pardon?" Abigail asked with an arched brow.

"I'm not suggesting we go skinny-dipping—although I must say the idea has great appeal,'' Luke said with a roguish grin.

Abigail had to agree, although she was surprised at herself for entertaining such thoughts.

Luke continued, ''I have a friend who'll provide swimsuits at the place I'm suggesting we go.''

''Now I'm intrigued,'' Abigail said. ''You mean you aren't going to spirit me off to a frigid mountain stream?''

''Not hardly. If you grew up in Bozeman, you must have heard of the hot springs at Chico,'' he said.

''I've heard about them, but I've never been there.''

''There's not much to see—a restaurant and bar built around a pool that's filled with water from a natural hot spring, so you can swim all year round. It's all tucked in a little niche in Paradise Valley, south of here.''

Abigail thought of Luke wearing nothing more than a pair of swimming trunks.

Luke imagined Abigail in nothing more than a form-fitting swimsuit.

"I have to admit it sounds like it might be fun," Abigail remarked.

Luke put a hand on the small of her back, urging her into her pickup. "Come on. I'll drive."

"You realize I'll probably regret this tomorrow," Abigail said.

"How so?"

"Dawn comes early when I'm on the job."

"I won't keep you up too late. Besides, this will relax all those tight muscles you've gotten climbing up and down mountainsides for the past two days."

It took almost an hour to get to Chico, where Luke quickly found his friend, the chef at the restaurant, and obtained suits for himself and Abby. She barely got a look at the tiny white French-cut swimsuit before Luke showed her into the dressing room to slip it on.

Abigail stared at herself in the mirror of the dressing room. The tank-style swimsuit left absolutely nothing to the imagination. Maybe if she were quick enough she could slip into the water before Luke got a good look. Her skin prickled from the cold the instant she stepped outside into the chilly night air.

"You'd better hurry up and get in," he said.

Luke's appreciative gaze warmed her, and she felt a coiling sensation in her belly. His eyes focused on her breasts, and her nipples hardened into tight buds that strained against the slick fabric.

As quickly as she could, Abigail slipped into the pool, actually sighing aloud in pleasure as the warm water covered her to the shoulders. Steam rose near the surface as the hot water met the cold air.

"This is wonderful," she murmured to Luke as he swam through the water to her side. "It's everything you promised and more."

"I can't believe what you were hiding under that old flannel shirt," Luke said, openly admiring her.

His heated gaze made Abigail's blood simmer. Looking for a way to defuse the situation, she said in a teasing voice, "My, what big eyes you have, Mr. Granger."

For a moment she was afraid Luke wouldn't remember the tale of Little Red Riding Hood and take his cue, but he grinned and promptly replied, "The better to see you with, my dear."

Abigail smiled in response. For the life of her she couldn't remember what came next. So she improvised, "My, what big... hands you have, Mr. Granger."

Luke stalked closer to her through the shallow water. Suddenly he reached out and captured her in his arms. With a smug grin he announced, "The better to catch you with, my dear."

Abigail laughed, but it was a decidedly breathless sound. When she saw Luke's eyes were filled with mirth, she felt safe saying, "My, what a furry chest you have, Mr. Granger."

She laid her hand on the black curls above his heart. She felt his muscles tense under her fingertips. His lips curled in a sensuous smile that revealed white teeth in the moonlight, reminding Abigail of another of the lines from the fairy tale. In an attempt to get things back to a more humorous vein she said, "My, what big teeth you have, Mr. Granger."

There was a long pause. Finally in a very quiet voice he answered, "The better to bite you with, my dear."

This time it was Abigail who tensed. She stood perfectly still as Luke slowly lowered his head to her shoulder and grazed her flesh with his teeth. A ripple of pleasure ran down her spine.

Abigail would have given a lot for the appearance of the fairy-tale woodchopper with his ax. Instead, she tore herself from Luke's grasp with a nervous laugh and fled with a strong, splashing kick toward the lighted area at the deep end of the pool. Luke wasn't as likely to try to make love to her there, where they could be plainly seen from the picture windows of the bar. An audience would surely deter his amorous overtures.

Or so she thought.

Abigail was still breathing hard when Luke caught up to her at the far end of the pool. He didn't give her the opportunity to escape him again. One hand slipped around her waist, pulling her up snug against him, so their practically naked bodies were flush, their legs entwined in the warm water, while his other hand reached for the edge of the pool to keep them afloat. He nudged her up against the tile wall and held her there with the length of his body, putting one hand on either side of her on the edge of the pool, effectively trapping her there.

Abigail gasped. ''Luke. There are people watching. We can't—''

He cut her off with a kiss, his lips claiming hers with an urgency that she quickly matched, her hands slipping around his neck to pull him close. His hips pressed against hers, and she could feel his arousal. She ended the kiss, leaning her head against his shoulder, trying to get her rioting senses back under control.

''I don't usually do this with an audience,'' she said.

''Me, neither,'' he answered with a crooked grin. Under the water, out of sight, one of his hands slid slowly upward along her ribs until he finally cupped her breast, the budding tip pressing against the palm of his hand.

Abigail didn't want the pleasure to end. But she knew that any minute someone might come out onto the pool area from the bar and see them. That thought made her put her hand atop his. "Luke, you have to stop. Someone might see us. Someone will—"

"No one can see what I'm doing, Abby. Just keep talking and—"

A masculine voice jolted them when it spoke practically beside them. "Hey, Luke. I thought that was you."

Luke pulled Abigail closer, hiding the state of their joint arousal from the sight of the intruder. "Hello, Nathan. Fancy meeting you here."

Abigail hid her face against Luke's chest. She heard the frustration in Luke's voice, but silently blessed Nathan Hazard for the timely interruption. To her chagrin, she'd been all too easily ensnared by the sexual lure Luke had thrown out to her.

"Who's that with you?" Nathan asked.

There was a brief hesitation before Luke said, "It's Abby."

"Abby?"

"Abigail Dayton," Luke bit out.

"From Fish and Wildlife?" Nathan asked, astonished.

"Yes, Nathan," Abigail said, realizing there was no sense hiding her head like an ostrich in the sand. She turned to face him. "It's me. Luke and I are relaxing a few tired muscles."

Nathan grinned. "Yeah. Sure."

A female voice called from the doorway. "Nathan?"

Luke turned to look, but the light was behind the woman, her face invisible in the shadows. She was wearing an off-the-shoulder dress with a skirt made of some filmy kind of material. The light behind her showed off a fantastic figure and a dynamite pair of legs. He turned back to his friend. "Who's that with you?"

"Uh..."

The woman stepped out into the pool area and made her way over to them. "Nathan, is it Luke? Oh, hello. It is you. Nathan thought he recognized you.''

It was Luke's turn to stare. ''Harry?''

Harriet Alistair smiled. ''Nathan tried to convince me to take a swim, but I was too chicken. How's the water?'' she asked Abigail.

''Marvelous,'' Abigail replied. She was stunned to see Harry and Nathan together, all animosity between them apparently forgotten. She was afraid to ask them how they'd solved their differences for fear of raising an issue that might put them at each other's throats again.

Luke was not so subtle. ''I thought you two hated each other's guts.''

Nathan stuck a hand in the trouser pocket of his Western suit pants. ''Uh. We called a truce for tonight.''

''Just for tonight?'' Abigail inquired.

''Nathan promised me a dinner of the best rack of lamb in two counties. I was willing to forego killing him for the pleasure,'' Harry said, throwing a quick smile in Nathan's direction.

"Why don't you two dry off and join us for a drink?" Nathan invited.

Luke glanced longingly at Abigail. It was obvious the other couple wasn't going to leave them alone. He was tempted to excuse himself and Abby and retreat to the privacy of the truck. But he had a feeling he wouldn't find the same Abby waiting for him once she was wearing jeans and a flannel shirt again.

He dreaded the thought of spending the next hour sitting on the opposite side of the truck from her, smelling her, feeling her presence, seeing her soft, smooth skin, and knowing all the time that when they arrived home they would most likely retire to their separate beds. They might as well stay and have a drink with Harry and Nathan. The later he and Abby started home, the more tired he would be when they got there, and the better he would sleep—if he ever fell asleep with her just across the hall.

"Fine," Luke said at last. He gave Nathan a penetrating stare, and his friend picked up on Luke's hint.

"Why don't we go inside and wait for

Luke and Abby,'' he said, taking Harry's arm and leading her back toward the bar.

"We'll join you soon," Abigail promised. She turned back to Luke and said, "This seems to be a pretty popular spot for seduction. Do you come here often?''

Luke paused so long before answering, that Abigail decided she didn't want to hear his answer. "It doesn't matter. I—''

"Wait, Abby.'' Luke caught her before she could swim away. "I've never been here to swim with another woman. I don't know why. I just—I guess I never thought it would be much fun. But with you, after what we did tonight…I mean the howling and all…I imagined being here with you would be exciting, exhilarating. And it was.''

His hand stroked across her bare shoulder. He grasped her nape and pulled her toward him. His mouth lowered to cover hers briefly, tantalizingly. "Ah, Abby. Everything is exciting with you.''

Abigail shivered, despite the heat of the water. She stared up into Luke's desire-darkened eyes, knowing that if she didn't

get away soon, she would be lost. She was
in danger of losing her heart to a man who
had no heart to give in return. She turned
and swam quickly to the ladder and climbed
out of the pool.

Luke watched her leave, wondering how
he'd ever let things go so far. What was
happening to him? When had he ever acted
so silly with a woman and enjoyed himself
so much? When had he ever had so much
fun with a woman who excited and tanta-
lized him at the same time?

Abigail Dayton wasn't like the other
women he'd known. But he was afraid to
trust what he'd found with her. It was too
good to be true. There had to be a catch
somewhere. So they'd done a little howling
at the moon together. So what? That was no
reason to let down barriers that had been up
for longer than he could remember.

"You still in the water?" Nathan
growled.

"What are you doing back out here?
Where's Harry?"

Nathan slumped into one of the wrought-iron chairs beside the pool. "She went home."

Luke levered himself out of the pool, grabbed the towel he'd left on a chair and began to dry off. "What the hell happened?"

"That fool woman is so thin-skinned—"

"What exactly did you say to her?"

"What could possibly be wrong with telling a woman she's attractive?" Nathan demanded.

"That's all you said? That she's an attractive woman?"

"I may have said something about her working too hard, because her hands were a little callused for a lady," Nathan admitted.

"What else?"

Nathan chewed on his lower lip in concentration. "I might have mentioned she shouldn't spend so much time in the sun, because her nose was freckled like a kid's."

"Anything else?" Luke asked dryly.

"I said she ought to sell her place to me and get back to being a woman."

Luke groaned.

"What was wrong with that?" Nathan asked belligerently.

Luke laughed and shook his head in disbelief. "If you don't know, Nathan, I don't think I can explain it to you."

"You can laugh at me all you want, so long as you give me a ride home."

"A ride?"

"The damned woman took my car when she left," Nathan grumbled.

Luke's laughter died. He couldn't very well leave Nathan stranded an hour's drive from home. But he'd looked forward to having Abigail to himself.

At that moment Abigail showed up dressed in her jeans and flannel shirt, her wet hair brushed back from her face. She looked so fresh and clean Luke wanted to put his cheek to hers and hold her close. He was suddenly very grateful for Nathan's presence.

There was something about Abigail Dayton that kept sneaking past defenses he'd kept strong for the past ten years. He would have to keep a careful watch on his feelings when he was around her, to make sure she didn't get past his guard. That way lay more trouble than he was willing to risk.

"Hi, Nathan. Luke. Where's Harry?" Abigail asked.

"She left," Nathan said flatly.

"Oh?"

"We're going to give Nathan a ride home," Luke said.

"Oh."

"Do you two still want to stay for a drink?" Nathan asked.

"I don't," Abigail said. "Do you, Luke?"

"No. We might as well head home."

Abigail was grateful for Nathan's presence in the pickup. Having a third person in the cab broke the tension between her and Luke. The more she talked to Nathan, the better she liked him. She wanted to ask him what had happened between him and Harry Alistair, but discretion kept her silent. She sincerely hoped he and Harry would work out their differences.

By the time they dropped Nathan off, Abigail was having a hard time keeping her eyes open. She leaned her head back against the leather seat, and against her will, her mind drifted back to her time in the pool with Luke. The touch of his hand, the taste of his mouth, the hard feel of his body against the softness of hers. Abigail turned her head to study Luke.

"See anything you like?"

"I like everything I see," she said. "I had a lovely time, Luke. Thank you for taking me."

Luke pulled the truck to a stop in front of his ranch house. "It was my pleasure, Abby."

Luke knew he should get out of the truck immediately, but he liked the way she was looking at him. He liked the way her low, sultry voice sounded in his ears. He liked Abigail Dayton way too much. He leaned over and pressed his lips to hers.

Abigail was expecting the kiss, and yet she was still surprised by the thrill she experienced at the firm touch of his mouth and the gentle caress that followed as his lips brushed hers. She kissed him back, capturing his lower lip in her teeth and nibbling gently, then letting her tongue trace the edge of his mouth. She felt the tension building, the need, the want.

And the fear that kept her from giving more.

Luke had never been kissed like this by a woman, with such restraint, when he was sure she wanted more, needed more. He wanted what she withheld. He wanted all of her. His mouth came seeking again, his tongue came searching, for what, he wasn't even sure.

Abruptly Abigail sat up, tearing her mouth from Luke's. "I have to go inside." She shoved open the door to the pickup and headed quickly toward the ranch house, with Luke on her heels.

"Abby."

The call of his voice sent her scurrying. She reached the back door to Luke's house and shoved it open. It was warm and welcoming inside, but she didn't stop to enjoy the atmosphere, just fled up the stairs two at a time toward the second floor and the safety of her room.

Luke caught her in the upstairs hallway and enfolded her in his embrace. Abigail didn't fight him, just dropped her forehead to his chest and waited for him to speak.

"Why are you running from me?" he asked in a ragged voice.

"I don't want to feel the things you make me feel, Luke. I don't want to leave a part of myself here when I go."

Luke didn't know what to say to that.

"Let me go, Luke."

He stepped away, letting his hands fall to his sides. "You have to live for today, Abby," he said. "We may not have tomorrow."

"That's the big difference between us," Abigail said. "You can't imagine a relationship with tomorrows. I can't imagine a relationship without them."

Abigail left Luke standing in the hall and closed the door to her bedroom firmly behind her. The differences between them were too great. He was like the renegade she sought, an independent creature, destined to travel the paths of life alone.

She needed more from a man. She wanted what she'd had with Sam. Luke could never give her that, so she had to stay away from him. Her very life depended on it.

7

When stalking, the wolf sneaks as close to the prey as it can without making it flee.

Sometime during a sleepless night, Abigail made up her mind to keep Luke at a stiff arm's length from now on. She'd enjoyed herself the previous evening much too much. It would be dangerous to let things progress to their natural conclusion. Abigail shivered at the thought of her naked skin pressed close to Luke's, of his hands on her breasts and belly.

In the past, Sam's face had intruded on such thoughts, saving her from folly. All she saw now were Luke's gray eyes, burning with desire for her.

Abigail smelled bacon cooking as she descended the stairs for breakfast. Surprisingly her appetite didn't seem to have suffered. She was starving. She dropped a large collection of gear in the living room before she headed for the kitchen.

"You look bright-eyed and bushy-tailed this morning, Miss Abigail," Shorty greeted her. "Have a seat, and I'll pour you some coffee. Bacon's ready, just need to drop some bread in the batter, and French toast is coming right up."

"Where's Luke?"

Shorty gave Abigail a speculative look as he handed her a mug of coal-black coffee. "He's up and gone."

"Gone?" Abigail felt bereft and grimaced at her fickle feelings.

"Said he'd be back 'fore you was to leave, and not to worry."

"I wasn't worried," she said too quickly, confirming for Shorty that she had been.

"Heard Luke whistling this morning," Shorty commented.

"Oh?"

"Don't whistle less'n he's happy. You must be good for him."

"Don't look for what isn't there, Shorty," Abigail warned, pouring maple syrup onto the golden French toast the old man had set in front of her.

Shorty served up a plate of French toast for himself and sat down at the table across from Abigail. "You denying you're attracted to Luke?"

Abigail fidgeted nervously with her fork. "That's none of your business."

"I don't want Luke hurt," Shorty said, his gaze intent on the French toast he was cutting up. "Luke's wife dragged him up, down and sideways over the years they was married. Didn't think he'd ever let himself care for another woman."

The implication Abigail heard was that Luke cared for her. But Shorty was wrong. That was the whole problem, as she saw it. Luke wasn't about to let himself care for a woman...any woman. The best way to protect herself from getting hurt was to stay away from him. "I think you're mistaken about Luke's feelings," she said.

Shorty looked up, his solemn eyes intent on her. "Don't hardly think so."

They were interrupted by the sound of

the front door opening. "What's all this
stuff?" Luke called from the living room.

Abigail was about to yell a reply when
Luke arrived at the doorway to the kitchen
and said, "You have enough stuff in here
to survive a month of Sundays in the wild."

Shorty retrieved a plate of French toast
that he'd kept warm in the oven and said to
Luke, "Sit down and eat."

Luke wasn't the least bit hungry, but he
did as he was told, his eyes never leaving
Abigail's face. She was beautiful. Funny
how he hadn't noticed that when he first
met her. He smiled inwardly. Even funnier
how he hadn't thought she was his type. He
wanted her more than any other woman
he'd ever known. Luke knew he'd better get
his mind off Abigail or he'd end up having
to keep his napkin on his lap after he got
up from the table.

"Are you planning to haul all that gear
with you in the helicopter?" he asked.

"If I sight the wolf and can't get him
with the tranquilizer gun, I plan to have the
copter pilot set me down as close to the

wolf as possible, so I can track him on foot.''

"Hope you packed some warm clothes. Weather report says there might be snow," Luke said.

"I've got everything I need," Abigail replied. "You don't have to worry about me."

"It's my old bones I'm thinking about," Luke said with a grin. "I'd better go pack some long johns."

"There's no need for you—"

He was out of the kitchen and up the stairs before Abigail had a chance to voice her objection. How could she feel threatened by a man who grinned like that? But she did. The grin was a tiny facet of the charming man who was urging her to succumb to his desires. Abigail simply had to resist that charm.

"He's a good man to have along on a hunt," Shorty said as he cleared the table.

"Except he seems more interested in hunting a two-legged species than in tracking the wolf," Abigail muttered. She heard the distant whir of the helicopter and rose to carry her plate to the sink.

"You 'member what I said," Shorty reminded as he took the plate out of her hands. "You take care of that boy. He's got a patched-up heart inside that big chest of his, make no mistake about it."

Abigail sighed. "You don't play fair, Shorty."

Shorty chortled. "Ain't fair to get as old as I am, either. But it sure beats my other choice all to heck."

That made Abigail laugh, and she kissed the old man on his weathered cheek. "I've got to go. You take care of yourself. Don't worry about me." Then, because she'd been affected by what he'd said, amended, "Us. Don't worry about us." She kissed him quickly on the other cheek and hurried out of the room.

Shorty concentrated on the sudsy dishwater, as though the two bright pink spots on his cheeks didn't exist. That sweet woman was going to make Luke a good wife. If he knew Luke, wolf or no wolf, it would all be decided before they came down out of those mountains.

Abigail ran smack into a broad chest at the kitchen door, and Luke's arms wrapped around her to keep her from falling. There they were, breast to breast, with the sun barely up in the sky. So much for keeping Luke at arm's length, Abigail thought as a shiver skittered down her spine. She stared up into Luke's face and watched a smile form, revealing the attractive dimple in his cheek. Lord, the man positively reeked with charm.

"The helicopter's here," Abigail said. "We have to go."

"I heard it," Luke answered. But he didn't release her.

Abigail pushed against his chest, seeking freedom. "It's time to go, Luke."

It was the fear in her voice, rather than what she said or did, that made Luke drop his arms and step back, allowing Abigail through the doorway. She hurried past him and began to gather up equipment in the living room. He crossed his arms over his chest and leaned back against the frame of the doorway, watching her. She was moving quickly, efficiently, but make no mistake about it, she wanted out of his house. And away from him.

Well, he wasn't going to let her get away. He would give her a little space, if that was what she needed. But they were going to be together, sooner or later. He didn't mind waiting a little while. She could run as much as she wanted, but he would follow. Eventually she would discover, and accept, that there was no escape.

"Hi, Geoff," Abigail greeted the copter pilot. The door had been taken off on the passenger's side. A web rope across the opening and a belt around her waist were all that would keep her from falling when she leaned out the door to use her tranquilizer gun. The lack of restraint had frightened her the first few times she'd gone up. Actually, it frightened her every time. But it was part of her job, so she suffered through it.

Luke had his own misgivings about the danger involved in what Abby was about to do, but he took his cue from her. She seemed confident she could handle the situation. He wasn't about to let her see his fear for her.

She started to lift her bags through the open space where there should have been a door, into the back of the copter, but Luke took them from her and did it himself. He helped her into the seat next to the pilot, then lifted his own things inside and settled himself into the seat behind her. A moment later they were in the air and wearing radio headsets so they could talk to one another.

Almost immediately, Abigail turned back to Luke to point out a large herd of mule deer grazing on his land alongside his sheep and realized that among the gear stacked beside him was a hunting rifle. "Why did you bring that gun?"

Luke unbuckled his seat belt and sat forward as he answered her. "There are other dangers in the mountains besides wolves, Abby. We may need it."

She didn't agree, but she didn't argue. Instead, she turned back around and directed Geoff where she wanted him to go, using a grid map on which she'd sectioned off the areas around the confirmed wolf kill.

Geoff angled the helicopter sharply as he banked for a turn, and one of Luke's bags started to fall out through the open space on Abigail's side. Luke took one look at the disappearing bag and realized the *condoms* were in there.

Abigail was startled when she saw the bag sliding toward the copter doorway. Before she could react, Luke made a death-defying grab for the bag and only caught it when half his body was hanging out of the copter. Her heart leapt to her throat when it seemed he was going to fall out.

Geoff saw what was happening and banked the opposite way. With corded muscles rippling in his back and shoulders, Luke made a superhuman effort to pull himself back inside the copter. An instant later it was all over. Luke was safe in his seat, the bag clasped to his side.

Abigail was furious. "You could have been killed!" she yelled. "What's in that bag that makes it worth dying for?"

Luke couldn't help the grin that split his

face. "Medical supplies," he shouted back. "*Necessary* medical supplies."

When Luke laughed, Abigail realized the man had thoroughly enjoyed every second of danger. It was a good thing she didn't love him. The woman who did was in for a lifetime of such hair-raising adventures. Abigail envied her every moment of it.

She turned back around in her seat and concentrated on looking for the wolf, which was, after all, the reason she'd come here in the first place. A few minutes later, Abigail saw the remains of a half-eaten deer. She leaned back and spoke to Luke. "Looks like this renegade likes deer better than he does sheep."

"Let's hope so," Luke replied.

They'd been in the air over an hour when Abigail sighted the wolf. "There he is!" Although her voice was excited, she kept her actions calm. She'd spent most of the trip with the tranquilizer gun in her lap, loaded and ready for action, knowing she might have to act fast.

They knew when the wolf felt threatened, because it began to run. Ordinarily there were enough treeless spaces, firebreaks and meadows, that Abigail would be able to tranquilize a wolf as it ran across an open area. Unfortunately this renegade stayed in the low brush, never giving her a clean shot.

"He's done this before," Luke murmured.

"What?" Abigail said distractedly.

"Look at him," Luke said, his voice full of admiration. "He knows we're trying to get him to bolt into the open. And he isn't going to do it. Abby, that is one smart wolf."

"He's going to be one smart *dead* wolf, if I can't reach him. Animal Damage Control won't need to get close to put a bullet in him."

"We'll catch him, Abby," Luke reassured her, laying a hand on her shoulder. "It just doesn't look like he's going to make it easy for us."

It was amazing how comforting Abigail found the touch of Luke's hand. Such a little thing. In that instant the feelings of loneliness she'd endured since Sam's death vanished. Abigail felt almost sick when she realized what that must mean. It wasn't smart to care so much for a man who wouldn't care for her. She jerked away from his touch, making sure he knew she wanted free of him.

Luke was confused by her rejection. And, though he would never have admitted it, he was also hurt.

Abigail was immediately sorry for over-reacting but was saved from destroying whatever she'd accomplished by pulling away, when Luke settled back into his seat.

They followed the wolf long enough to be sure he wasn't going to break into the open. Finally Abigail said to Geoff, "Look for a meadow, someplace open where you can get the copter down. I'll have to track this wolf on foot. Tell my office I'll be out of touch until I catch him."

Soon after that, Luke and Abigail were waving Geoff off and distributing between themselves the supplies Abigail had brought.

"I'll carry that," Luke said, when Abigail put the two-man dome tent in her pack. She started to argue but merely shrugged and let him have it. He was bigger and stronger. He could carry more. They were both toting heavy loads when everything was divided, but Abigail was used to it. "We'll head toward the last sighting and pick up the trail there."

Luke didn't question the way Abigail took the lead. He found himself admiring her determination as much as he admired the wiliness of the wolf that eluded her. It would be interesting to observe Abigail's tactics with the wolf. He was bound to learn something about capturing an elusive spirit that might be useful to him in his pursuit of Abby.

Abigail shivered as a blast of Arctic air hit the sweat on the back of her neck. The weather was already turning frigid, a forerunner of the promised snow. "I don't think the snow will be entirely a bad thing," she remarked. "It'll certainly make tracking the wolf easier."

Luke smiled wryly. It would take quite an optimist to find something good about being on foot in the mountains with a storm threatening. The lowering gray storm clouds were considerably worse by the time he suggested they think about setting up a camp.

Abigail shook her head no. Panting with the uphill climb, she replied, "The wolf will look for a place to sit this out. I'd like to find him before he goes to ground."

Luke saw it first, a gray shadow in the undergrowth. "Abby," he whispered.

She followed his pointing finger and found what she'd been searching for—a gray wolf. He was magnificent, nearly six feet from the tip of his nose to the tip of his tail and about a hundred pounds, Abby estimated. The wolf's pelt was a light gray, with darker fur along the center of his back and tail. His legs, ears and muzzle were tawny.

Despite the fact wolves rarely threatened humans, Abigail hadn't forgotten that a wolf's fangs could be more than two inches in length, and its powerful bite was capable of ripping through four inches of moose hide and hair, or snapping off the tail of a full-grown steer as cleanly as a knife. Abby hadn't realized she was holding her breath until she released it in a rush.

She slowly eased her pack down off her shoulders and took the tranquilizer gun in both hands, sighting down the scope. In that instant, the wolf lifted its head.

"He knows we're here," Luke said in a quiet voice.

"One...more...second...." Abigail squeezed gently on the trigger.

The wolf bolted the instant she fired. A second later he'd disappeared into the forest.

"Missed! Damn it, I missed!" Abigail was furious with herself. The hunt would be all over now if only she'd hit what she'd aimed at.

"He was already spooked," Luke said. "You didn't have much of a shot before he ran."

"But I did have a shot," Abigail said. "And I missed."

"Every hunter misses now and then."

"I don't. Not very often, anyway," she conceded. "Now that he's running we probably won't get another chance at him before the storm hits.'' Her grip tightened on the gun. ''I couldn't afford to miss.''

''No sense crying over spilled milk,'' Luke said practically.

Abigail tried to hang on to her anger. As long as she was angry she could refuse the much-needed comfort Luke was offering. Instead of answering him, she loaded up her pack and marched off after the wolf.

Luke shook his head at Abby's contrariness as he followed in her footsteps. ''Have you always been this hard on yourself?'' he asked as they headed farther up the mountain.

It would be completely churlish, almost childish, not to answer him. She dropped back to walk beside Luke and admitted, ''Ever since I was a little girl I've always wanted to be the best at whatever I did.''

''And were you?''

''Yes.'' When he arched a disbelieving brow she amended, ''At least, enough of the time that I got to be pretty sure of succeeding no matter what I tried to do.''

''Maybe I should be asking if you ever

failed at anything,'' Luke said with a wry twist of his mouth.

Abigail kept her face carefully blank as she said, ''A few things.'' She hadn't been able to keep the people she loved from dying. First her mother and father. Then Sam.

To avoid having to elaborate, she asked, ''How about you? Apparently you've been a pretty successful sheep rancher. Was there ever anything you really wanted that you didn't manage to get for yourself?''

''I have to admit, I usually get what I go after, too,'' Luke answered, catching her gaze and refusing to release it.

Abigail felt the threat, but was helpless to escape it.

Luke felt himself sinking into a bottomless well of emotion. He hadn't felt these feelings for years—if ever—and he didn't want to feel them now. The urge was there to say more to her, to admit that he hadn't been entirely truthful. He hadn't always gotten everything he'd wanted. He hadn't been very good at getting a woman to love him. Not his mother. Not his wife. Not any of the women he had known.

Without realizing it, they'd both stopped walking. Luke probed Abigail's eyes, as though he might find evidence of what lay in her heart. Here was a woman he thought might offer him the love he'd always wanted—if he gave her the chance.

But that didn't seem like such a smart thing to do. What if he was wrong? What if she was just like all the others? It was safer to take what he could get. They could share some good times together. When she was gone there would be others. There always were.

Abigail saw the kiss coming. She wanted it. Her body trembled in expectation. But she mustn't allow it to happen. She ducked her head as his mouth reached hers and headed away at a quick pace.

"We'd better keep moving," she said. "Once the snow starts falling we'll have to stop for the day. I want to cover as much ground as I can before then."

The next couple of hours were spent climbing in rugged terrain. Abigail followed the trail left by the wolf, which cut across the East Boulder River, ever closer to the summer pastures where Luke's sheep grazed. Luke moved with her like a shadow. She was aware that a virile male was stalking her, even as she stalked the wolf.

Luke's eyes rested often on Abigail, and whenever she looked over her shoulder to see if he followed, he made a point of letting her know he was there, watching, waiting for the opportunity to take what she'd avoided giving earlier. She would be his before the night was done.

Late in the afternoon, snow began falling in large, beautiful flakes that made the forest look like a winter wonderland.

Abigail stopped and stuck out her tongue to catch several flakes. "Umm. They're cold."

Luke watched as snowflakes gathered on her eyelashes and drifted across her cheeks. He wanted to kiss them off. As he closed the distance between them, her head jerked upright, and she stared warily at him. He fought to control the need, the desire to touch her. He didn't want to frighten her away. Take it one step at a time, he told himself. One small step at a time.

It was a magical snowfall. Slowly and silently the soft white powder blanketed the earth. Before long, Abigail was forced to concede that they weren't going to catch up to the wolf. "We might as well quit for the day," she said. "I saw a spot a few minutes back that might be a good place to camp."

"If you don't mind hiking another five minutes, there's a hunting cabin where we can spend the night," Luke said.

"With real beds?" Abigail said, her eyes lighting.

"A real bed and a couple of chairs in front of a wood stove," he replied with a smile.

"I'm sorry you had to haul that tent all day for nothing, but a roof and a stove sounds great to me. Lead on."

Night came swiftly in the mountains. By the time they arrived at the cabin, there was barely light to see.

"How charming!" Abigail said when she spotted the tiny A-frame cabin. She was even more pleased when she stepped inside. "Why, it's lovely. You didn't tell me it was so nice,'' she said. ''You even have running water!''

''It's a private getaway. A place where I can come to be by myself and think,'' Luke confessed.

Abigail looked around the cabin, with its rustic wooden bed and table and chairs, a black wood stove along one wall and a kitchen area along another. A tiny niche she saw held a bathroom with indoor plumbing—wonder of wonders! The cabin had everything needed for comfort in a single room. The curtains and the bedspreads were all a masculine red-and-black plaid. There was a bearskin beside the double bed. The wooden chairs in front of the stove faced a window through which it was still possible to see snow falling in the last rays of evening light.

''I can't believe this,'' Abigail said, shaking her head with astonishment. ''If I had a place like this, I'd never leave it.''

''If I had a woman like you to share it with me, I'd have no cause to leave it, either.''

Abigail lowered her eyes to hide her reaction to Luke's comment. She didn't want to be tempted. And being alone with Luke in this place was all too tempting.

Luke was startled by what he'd said, but realized it was the truth. Abigail filled a void he hadn't known existed. He had her in his lair. What was he going to do about it?

"Abigail," Luke said softly. "Come here."

8

*The stage of the hunt that immediately
follows the stalk is the encounter. This is the point
at which prey and predator confront each other.*

"I don't think that's a very good idea,"
Abigail said in a shaky voice.

"What are you afraid of, Abby? I won't
bite," Luke teased.

"I might," Abigail snapped back.

Luke eyed her as a predator might its
prey. He could see that Abigail felt the tension, too. The need. It was there, shimmer-
ing between them. He could wait. They
needed time to rest and to satisfy their physical hunger. Then they could concentrate on
the desire that arced between them. He was
already aroused just looking at her, antici-
pating what was to come. It was a sweet

ache and one which he hoped Abby would assuage before the night was done.

"We might as well get settled in before it gets any darker. I'll take care of the fire, if you'll handle dinner," Luke said.

Abigail was immediately suspicious. Luke was acting as though he hadn't just made a pass at her. He *had* made one, hadn't he? It hadn't been her imagination, had it? Oh, he was clever all right, pretending like he wasn't watching, like he'd given up the thought of touching her, tasting her, thrusting himself deep inside her. Abigail knew better. She wasn't about to let down her guard.

Luke laid a fire in the wood stove while Abigail fixed a pot of coffee. They both chose cold rations she'd brought along rather than having to cook and wash dishes.

Abigail moved warily around Luke, keeping her distance. But it wasn't a large cabin, and they kept brushing against each other. Every time they did, Abigail felt a frisson of excitement that left her wanting. Luke teased, he taunted, with the barest of touches, never enough that she could say, "Stop that," but enough to make her conscious of him, of what was to come.

At last they sat before the wood stove sipping a second cup of coffee. Abigail had her feet tucked up under her, almost relaxed, when Luke asked, "Did you ever do this with Sam?"

"Do what?" she asked.

"Spend the night together alone in the forest."

Abigail chose to make a joke of what he'd said, because to treat it seriously was too unsettling. "Sam and I spent a lot of time together in the forest," she said with a forced laugh. "After all, we were forest rangers."

"That's not what I meant."

"Maybe what you meant is none of your business," Abigail said.

"I'm making it my business," Luke replied, never taking his eyes off hers.

Abigail was feeling trapped again. She didn't understand why he was so interested in her relationship with Sam. She found it painful to dredge up those memories. But Luke's forceful gaze demanded it.

She took a deep breath and said, "Sam and I often camped together in the forest, usually in a tent. We both loved the sight of the stars and moon overhead when we...made love. Is that what you wanted to hear?"

It was what he'd expected—another eulogy to the memory of a perfect man. How could he possibly compete? Luke set his coffee cup on the small table beside his chair, threaded his hands together and leaned forward with his arms on his thighs. "I'm only a flesh-and-blood man, Abby, with all the faults and foibles we humans possess. I'm not perfect like Sam. But I want you. I want to share whatever the night brings with you."

The fact that Abigail was tempted to take him up on his offer left her shaken and defensive. "Sam had a heart. Sam was capable of loving. That's what made being with him special. I'm not willing to settle for less."

"I have a—" Luke clamped his teeth. He

didn't have to prove anything to her. But he wasn't willing to back down, either. "The truth is, that it's much safer to put yourself in the grave with Sam than to keep on living, isn't that it, Abby?"

Abigail's face paled. She carefully set her coffee cup on the table between them, to avoid the urge to throw it in his face. She struggled at the same time to get to her feet. "How dare you!"

She didn't know she was going to hit him until her hand had already streaked out. Luke rose and caught her wrist the instant before her palm reached his face. He pulled her around the table to confront him.

"Too close to the truth for comfort, Abby?" he said quietly. "You've put Sam on a pedestal and kept him there rather than let another man get close. Why is that, Abby?"

He caught her chin, so she had no choice except to meet his gaze. His eyes demanded the truth from her. "What's really holding you back, Abby?"

"I'm scared," she said at last. "I'm scared." Abigail had never acknowledged her fear to anyone in words—not even to herself. Admitting to Luke that she was afraid made her feel tremendously vulnerable.

Luke drew Abby into his arms. Her head rested on his shoulder as her body shuddered to contain sobs she refused to set free. "You don't have to be scared, Abby. I'm here. I won't let anything bad happen to you."

She clutched fistfuls of his shirt and said, "You don't understand. I don't want to love any man ever again—and lose him. I don't want to go through that kind of pain again. I couldn't bear it. Now do you understand?"

"I understand, Abby. I do." Luke held her in his arms, offering comfort, but she was inconsolable. "I'm not going to die, Abby," he murmured. "Not for a good long while, anyway." He was kissing her cheeks, her eyes, her forehead, caressing her back and shoulders with his hands.

"It's happened before," she said. "It could happen again." She tried to escape his embrace, to escape the pain and fear, but he wouldn't let her go.

"Are you telling me that I matter to you, Abby?"

"Oh, Luke."

He saw her answer in her eyes. At that moment, something happened inside him. The wall that had encased his heart crumbled, leaving him as vulnerable as the woman he held in his arms.

When Luke reached for the snap on Abby's jeans, her hand was there to stop him. He never took his eyes off her face, just moved her hand aside. Slowly, surely, he unsnapped her jeans and then unzipped them, pushing the material away so he could slide his hand down inside and cup the heart of her.

Abigail felt the heat pooling between her thighs. When her legs would no longer support her, she raised her arms to encircle Luke's neck.

"Luke," she whispered.

"What?"

She didn't say anything, simply began unsnapping his shirt, one pearl button at a time. She pulled the shirt out of his jeans along with the long johns underneath, exposing a chest full of black curls.

Luke hissed in a breath of air when she rubbed her cheek against his chest and gasped when she found a nipple with her teeth. An instant later he heard the snap on his jeans and watched as Abby's eyes were drawn to the line of dark, downy hair that ran from his navel downward.

Luke withdrew his hand and lifted her onto the thigh he thrust between her legs. His hands cupped her buttocks as he pulled her toward him. The pressure caused Abigail to groan.

Luke leaned his cheek against hers, and Abigail felt the harsh rasp of a day's growth of beard. She wanted this. She wanted him. But there were things that had to be considered before they allowed themselves to go any further.

"Luke, we have to be responsible," Abigail said with more regret than she realized he could hear. "We're out here in the middle of nowhere and, much as I'm tempted, it's better that we don't start something we can't finish. What I mean to say is, I have no more protection now than I had two days ago.''

"I do," Luke said.

Abigail swallowed hard. "You do?"

Luke nodded his head toward the bag that had nearly gone out the helicopter door.

"Oh, my God," she whispered, as realization dawned. "Medical supplies."

"*Necessary* medical supplies," he said with a wolfish grin. "There's plenty of protection, Abby. That doesn't have to stop us. But maybe there's some other reason—"

"There's nothing else, Luke. Except..." She was reluctant to admit that she was afraid she wouldn't meet whatever expectation he might have in a lover. Instead she said, "It's been a while since...I mean..."

Luke thrust his hands into her hair. "I know it's been a long time since you've made love, Abby." He leaned down to kiss the roses that appeared on each cheek. "I'll be gentle and take it slow, as slow as you want."

Abigail was too conscious of Luke's thigh between her legs, of his hand tangled in her hair, to think rationally. "Oh, Luke," she said. "I do want you, only…"

"Only what?"

"There are good reasons why we shouldn't do this."

Luke's thumbs caressed her temples as he asked, "Are you going to bring up that nonsense again about me dying?"

"It isn't nonsense," she said. "I don't want to care for anyone, Luke. I—"

He put his lips to hers to quiet her. "Shh. Shh. Take it easy. We'll talk about all that later. We have something else to do right now. I want to be close to you, Abby. I want to be deep inside you, touching a part of you I can't touch any other way."

Abigail tried for a smile, and though her lips quivered, she managed one. "I don't think this is a good idea. It's not you, Luke. I mean, if I were going to do this with anyone, it would be you.…"

"That's good to hear."

"But since Sam died, I haven't wanted to make love to anyone."

Luke gathered her hands into his own. "I'm not asking for your love, Abby," he said in a quiet voice. His hands tightened to keep her from speaking. "I want something entirely different from you."

"Sex," Abigail said.

"Yes, sex." There was more he wanted from her. But he wasn't going to ask for it.

Abigail thought about what he had said, and what he hadn't. He wasn't offering love. And he didn't expect it in return. Abigail didn't let her head make the decision; she left it to her heart. She took a deep breath and said, "All right, Luke."

Abigail had thought she knew what she was doing. When they stood naked in the firelight before each other, she wasn't so sure. She trembled as Luke's callused fingers caressed her bare shoulder, followed by his mouth in the hollow above her collarbone. His hands caught her waist, and his searching fingers slipped up onto her ribs, his thumbs tracing them from center to edge and back again. His fingertips moved upward, circling her breasts, teasing again, but leaving her unsatisfied.

Abigail's hands found the fur pelt on Luke's chest, and she dug her fingers into the black curls. She leaned into him, scraping her flesh deliciously against his skin.

Luke held her close, enjoying the feel of their two bodies aligned from breast to thigh. His hands cupped her buttocks and pulled her close, and he leaned into the embrace, wanting to be closer still.

"This is torture," Luke said, his forehead resting against hers. "I can't touch you enough, can't hold you enough. Can't—"

Abigail's hands framed his face, lifting it until she could see the fierce wanting in his eyes. "Touch me, Luke. Hold me. I want you so much."

His lips captured hers, his tongue plundering her mouth, taking what he wanted, what he needed. He stopped kissing her long enough to lift her into his arms, make a brief detour to collect the necessary protection, and carry her to bed, where he quickly joined her on the flannel sheets.

Sensations. Abigail reveled in them. Smooth skin over hard muscle. Sweat and heat. Controlled power. The gentleness of a strong man's caress.

Sensations. Luke had never known a woman who affected him as she did. Softness. Curves that fit in his hands. Dampness and heat. A woman's tenderness that reached deep inside him to warm the coldness there.

"Abby, Abby, let me inside."

He opened a foil packet, but she took it from him. "Let me." Slowly, using both hands, she led him to the center of her desire and guided him inside. Suddenly, she was filled with him.

A deep, guttural groan of pleasure and satisfaction rose from his chest.

"Oh, Luke." Abby's voice was filled with awe. "I feel so full. It...it feels so good."

She held him close, trying to touch enough, to taste enough to last a lifetime, though the fire between them raged so hot she was certain nothing could ever put it out.

The tension built as they performed the dance of wolves, the ritual of mating.

"Give yourself to me, Abby."

"Luke, kiss me, please."

"Here, Abby. Touch me here."

"Luke, hold me. Love me."

"Abby, baby, I can't wait much longer...."

"Sweetheart, I can't wait...."

Then they were flying, soaring together, their bodies arched, shuddering with ecstasy. It was a trip to the heavens, a visit to a paradise that few ever know, two souls joined as their bodies find in each other their perfect human complement.

Abigail lay gasping for breath. Luke lay beside her, his broad chest rising and falling in an effort to catch up to his racing pulse.

It was never like this with Sam. The thought came before Abigail could repress it. And with it the knowledge that what she felt for Luke, what she had felt from virtually the first moment she'd seen him, was far stronger than what she'd experienced with Sam, whom she'd known nearly all her life. She wanted to cry. She wanted to shout hosanna. She closed her eyes and lay perfectly still, as though to deny the emotions roiling inside her.

It was never like this with any other

woman. Luke knew he'd found more than sexual fulfillment in Abby's arms. He was terrified. He was ecstatic. He couldn't marry her. He couldn't let her go. He didn't know what to do.

At that moment, Abigail turned her back to him, and he knew that whatever he felt, whatever he decided for the long term, at this moment he wanted to hold her in his arms. He turned on his side and pulled her close, to spoon her against him.

''Luke, I—''

He cut her off with the pressure of his hand on her belly. ''Don't say anything tonight, Abby. Just sleep. We'll talk about this in the morning.''

He knew she must be feeling as excited, upset and confused about what had happened between them as he did. Something special *had* happened between them. But if he admitted his feelings to Abby tonight, she'd have a hold on him that he couldn't escape. He didn't trust the love he felt. It had betrayed him before.

''Go to sleep, Abby.''

Abigail clenched her jaw. She hadn't expected a declaration of love. And he hadn't disappointed her. She certainly wasn't going to shed any tears over him. It was better this way. It would hurt to lose him now, but not as much as it would hurt if she let him into her life.

Something warm and hot fell on Luke's arm, the one he had around Abby. A tear. She was crying. He tried to harden his heart against her pain. He'd done it before with other women. He could do it again.

Only this time, things were different. This time, he felt her pain.

He turned Abigail in his arms and tucked her head under his chin, holding her close, feeling his body heating again, even though it had been so recently sated.

"All right, Abby. I'll say it." Angrily he admitted, "I care for you. Is that what you wanted to hear? But it isn't going to change anything. I won't marry you. I'm never going to marry again. I'm not cut out for it. When you catch this renegade wolf, when you're finished here, that's it. We part ways."

He wasn't going to use the word love.

Love had never been a good thing in his life. Abby would have to settle for caring. It was the best he could offer.

Abigail heard what Luke had said. And what he had not said. "I'll take what I can get," she whispered.

Her lips caressed his neck, his chest, his cheek, his eyelids, and finally his mouth. It was a kiss that expressed her love, the love he didn't want...and refused to return.

The banked fires between them burst into flame and burned hot again. Their hands roamed, seeking out the places they'd learned could give pleasure.

"Luke, Luke, stop," Abigail begged in a breathless voice.

"What? What's wrong?" Luke had trouble rising from the well of pleasure into which she had taken him.

"I...uh..."

"What is it, Abby?"

She hid her face against his chest and said, "I've always wanted to make love on a bearskin rug. Do you suppose..."

The rich sound of masculine laughter filled the cabin. "Say no more."

An instant later, Abigail's buttocks were lying nestled on the bearskin rug beside the bed, and Luke's body mantled hers.

"Now, where were we?" Luke asked with a roguish grin.

"I believe you were making love with me. Your mouth was right here." Abigail pointed to the hollow above her collarbone.

"So I was," Luke said, his mouth lowering to her skin.

Abigail groaned, a harsh sound that grated up from deep within her. It was the first of many sounds of pleasure that followed throughout the night.

9

*The chase is the stage of the hunt
in which the prey flees and the wolf follows.*

Abigail had lied to Luke. Simply knowing he cared was not enough. She wanted everything he had to give. She wanted his love.

Despite all the precautions she'd taken over the past three years not to get involved, she had, in a matter of days, fallen into a trap she hadn't seen until its jaws had closed around her. She should have been more wary. The consequences of loving were frightening, and Luke had already told her the price she would have to pay for her foolishness. Contemplation of a life without him left her feeling desolated.

She forced herself to concentrate on tracking the wolf. Once her work was done she could escape the pain of loving a man who refused to love her back.

The weather was considerably warmer, all the way up in the mid-sixties, making it a pleasure to walk in the mountains. They had picked up wolf sign early, and Abigail had high hopes they would find the renegade today. The snow was melting quickly under a warm sun, and there were only patches of white to be found.

What attracted Abigail's eyes was a patch of snow stained yellow. She went on one knee and scooped her gloved hand down under the top layer of snow. She carefully brought a handful of the stained snow up to her nose, which wrinkled when it caught a pungent scent.

"I assume you did that for a purpose," Luke said, eyeing her askance. "What did you find out?"

"The wolf was here." She held the snow out for him to sniff, and as he did she explained, "Elk and deer smell like the grass and trees they eat, pleasant. Wolves smell rank and gamy."

"Definitely wolf," Luke agreed with a wrinkle of his nose.

Abigail dropped the snow and dusted her gloved hand against her jeans. "He's not far ahead of us."

Her words proved to be true. They both spotted the wolf at the same instant, but Luke was quicker to react. The picture of the wolf poised over the dead carcass of one of his sheep spurred him to action. He had his rifle raised and aimed, his finger tight on the trigger, when Abigail's cry of horror made him pause.

"Stop! Don't shoot. Please, Luke." Her hand gripped his arm, tightening as he sighted down the barrel.

Luke's jaw worked as he gritted back the fury he felt toward the fleeing wolf, which was threatening his livelihood. He made the mistake of looking at Abigail, and the pleading expression in her wide green eyes caused him to swing his rifle away in disgust.

Abigail breathed a sigh of relief and brought her shaking hand up to rake it through her disheveled blond hair. "Thank you," she said.

"For what?" he spat. "You're running out of time, Abby. That renegade isn't going to let you catch him. Some wild things can't be caged. The only way to stop him is to put a bullet in him."

"I'm not giving up!" Abigail replied in a voice made more fierce by the fact that she feared he was right. "I'll catch him, and I'll cage him. He is not a lost cause, Luke."

Any more than you are, she thought. She was not a quitter. She wasn't going to give up on the wolf. She wasn't going to give up on Luke, either. He was capable of loving. She just had to convince him of that fact.

Luke wasn't sure what to make of the determined look in Abby's eyes or her militant stance, with her hands fisted on her hips. But he didn't intend to argue with her. He simply stalked off toward the dead sheep, with Abigail hard on his heels.

When they got a good look at the sheep carcass and examined all the evidence to be found, it was Abigail's turn to rant. "It's a good thing you didn't shoot, because that wolf didn't kill this sheep!'' she said. ''Most likely it was coyotes. Now, aren't you glad I stopped you?''

Luke saw Abby was expecting an apology. But he wasn't going to give it to her. He hadn't said anything he didn't still believe. ''Maybe that renegade didn't kill this sheep, but he's sure developing a fine taste for mutton. You better find him, Abby, and find him quick. If I get my sights on him again—''

''You'll hold your fire like you did this time,'' Abigail cut in. ''My ten days aren't up, Luke. If you shoot that wolf—which I'll remind you is a *protected* endangered species—I'm going to see that you're prosecuted to the full extent of the law.''

''So, my innocent little lamb is a big, bad wolf in disguise,'' Luke murmured with a reluctant grin. ''All right, Agent Dayton. Lead on. This wolf hunt is getting downright interesting.''

By sundown, another of Abigail's precious ten days was gone, and she hadn't done more than catch another brief glimpse of the wolf she'd come to trap.

That evening, they found a nice level spot in an open area where they could set up the tent. Fortunately the weather was in the low fifties, comfortable enough for sleeping outdoors. It was the sleeping *arrangements* that Abigail was finding awkward. Luke insisted it made sense to zip their two sleeping bags together.

''The space inside the tent is small enough that we'll both be more comfortable if we make one bed that fills the whole space,'' he explained.

Abigail didn't argue, but not because she thought what he said made any sense. She wanted to lie close to Luke. She wanted to savor whatever time she had with him. She wanted a chance to convince him that they belonged together.

Luke wasn't sure what imp had prompted him to zip their sleeping bags together, but he couldn't be sorry for the result, as he watched Abby ease her jeans down her legs and slip between the down covers.

He'd spent the day in an agony of wanting her, knowing that she'd be leaving him soon to return to her life in Helena. Where she might meet another man. Where she might marry and have the children that ought to be his.

Luke's thoughts were both irritating and confusing. He didn't love her. He damn sure didn't want to marry her. Why should he care what happened to her after she left the valley?

He stripped down to his long johns and crawled into the sleeping bag beside Abby. Where he promptly recalled every delightfully sensuous moment of the previous night spent loving her. And realized that from the moment he'd wakened that morning, with the sound of Abigail singing in the tiny shower in his mountain cabin, he'd thought of little else but loving her again.

The howl of a wolf, sad and mournful, raised goose bumps on Abigail's arms. "That's him," she whispered in the darkness.

"Most likely," Luke agreed.

"He sounds so alone."

"I know how he feels."

"What did you say?"

Luke turned on his side toward Abigail. Enough moonlight filtered through the tent walls for him to see shapes, but no more. He reached out a hand and cupped her cheek. "I think maybe I've been lonely a long time, Abby. Only I didn't realize it until last night."

Abigail put her hand over Luke's and turned her head slightly so she could kiss his callused palm. "What was different about last night?"

"You filled a hole inside me that I didn't even know was there."

Abigail took Luke's hand in both of hers and brought it down to cup her breast. "Touch me, Luke. Take what you need."

The heavy swell of her breast in his hand felt right, it felt good. He caressed her, but there was too much cloth in his way. Slowly, giving her a chance to object, he began to unbutton her wool shirt. When it was off, he reached down and pulled her long john shirt up over her head. By the time he was finished, breathless moments later, he had stripped them both bare. He pulled her toward him, to feel the softness and the heat of her against his nakedness.

Abigail moaned as the tips of her breasts nestled in the crisp mat of hair that covered Luke's chest. She rubbed herself from side to side, enjoying the feel of their two bodies, hard and soft, brushing against each other.

Luke grasped her buttocks and pulled her belly against the part of him that was hard with need.

Her hand reached down to cup him and Luke groaned and put his hand against hers to hold her there. He was so soft and so hard, both at the same time, that Abigail delighted in the contrast.

"Luke?" she murmured.

"What, Abby?" he said breathlessly as his tongue laved the heavy pulse where her throat and jaw met.

"Did you remember to bring in...the... protection."

Luke smiled against her skin. "I have all the necessary medical supplies at hand," he assured her.

Abigail released a moan of pleasure as

Luke's tongue and teeth nipped her earlobe and then soothed the pain. There was an urgency to his loving that hadn't been there before—as though he might not have another chance, and he had to make enough memories to last forever.

His mouth trailed down from her throat to her breasts and from there to her navel. His tongue followed his hands as he reveled in the taste of her. His mouth found the fount of life and drank of the sweetness there.

Abigail gripped Luke's hair as her body rose up to meet his mouth and tongue. The sensations were unbelievable. She reached out to him with her body and with her soul, hoping he would take all she was offering.

"Luke, I want you inside me. Fill me up."

He did. And found himself fulfilled as well. Being inside her, moving inside her, his body joined with hers, as their hearts pounded in chests gasping for air, lifted him to some higher plane of being.

"Abby," he gasped. "Baby, slow down.

Not so fast. Make it last. Make it last forever.''

Abigail tried to make it last. But the rising tension wouldn't wait. Couldn't be stopped. It flowed up and over and around her, making her body tense like a tightly strung bow, until she thought she might snap. "Luke," she cried. "I can't bear it. It's too much."

Her face contorted with pleasure too great to bear. Her fingernails dug crescents in his back, and her legs clamped tight around his buttocks, refusing to release him, as she climaxed, shuddering again and again.

Luke thrust savagely inside her, wanting to be a part of the joy. He envied the sheen of happiness that bathed her glowing face.

Abby's arms grasped his nape and pulled him down to join her mouth to his, taking his soul, giving her soul in return.

Luke tensed and growled in guttural satisfaction as his body spilled its seed into hers. Then, exhausted, he lay upon her, as their bodies heaved to carry air to struggling lungs.

Abigail welcomed Luke's heavy weight atop her, but despite her protest, he rolled to his side and pulled her into his arms.

"Abby, Abby. It's so good between us. It's never been so good for me."

"I feel the same. It was—oh, Luke!" she wailed in sudden realization.

Luke jerked up, afraid he'd somehow hurt her. "What is it, Abby? What's wrong?"

"We forgot about protection."

"Protection?" He was only confused an instant before it dawned on him what she meant. There was no empty foil packet lying anywhere in the vicinity.

He rubbed his forehead in consternation. "Lord, Abby, I don't know what happened. I planned...I'm never irresponsible about things like that. I know better than to get caught in that kind of female trap—"

Abigail tore herself from his arms, rising quickly to her knees. "Don't worry," she said, both angry and hurt. "I wouldn't think of trying to trap you. I'm a big girl. I'm as responsible as you are for making sure 'mistakes' don't happen. So don't you worry about anything.''

She lay down in a huff and pulled the sleeping bag up over her shoulder.

Luke reached out a hand to touch her, and she yanked her shoulder away. ''Don't touch me. I'm tired. I want to go to sleep.''

Luke didn't know what to say. He'd really made a mess of things with Abby tonight. He wasn't the kind of man to forget something as important as protection. So what had gone wrong? The thought of his child growing inside her…it was something he hadn't realized how much he wanted.

Who had he been trying to force into a decision—himself, or Abby? He couldn't think about that right now. He'd be smart to get some sleep. He had a feeling tomorrow was going to be a very long day.

Luke was right about the very long day, which seemed even longer in the face of Abby's silence. She wasn't speaking to him except when absolutely necessary. They were close to the wolf. He could smell it, feel it. Any moment he expected to see the gray renegade again.

They heard the wolf before they saw it. It was battling another animal, and the vicious sounds coming from the throats of both beasts were frightening in their savagery.

Luke and Abigail approached the glade in the forest cautiously, Abby with her tranquilizer gun ready, Luke with his rifle in hand. When they reached the site of all the noise, they were treated to a stunning spectacle. The magnificent gray wolf was doing battle with a yearling grizzly bear, while in the background six wolf pups stood in the opening to a den, yipping with excitement.

"It's the renegade—and *he's* a *she*. A mother!" Abigail said, her heart pounding with excitement. It wasn't hard to figure out what had happened to cause the fight between the bear and the wolf. The wolf had buried a cache of uneaten meat near the den. The bear had apparently dug it up and been eating it when the wolf returned. Feeling her pups threatened, she'd attacked.

Abigail was stunned by the ferocity of the female wolf. Her teeth bared, she confronted the bear, which outweighed her by nearly two hundred pounds. What she lacked in weight, she made up in mobility, running circles around the bear, biting and retreating. But the bear wasn't going anywhere. It swiped at the wolf with deadly claws and revealed sharp canines of its own when the wolf snapped at it with powerful jaws.

Abigail looked at Luke, not sure what to do. If she tranquilized one animal and then missed her shot at the other, she'd be condemning one to a savaging by the other. Yet she now had the wolf in her sights—along with her six pups, and she couldn't let the three-toed renegade escape.

"I'll distract the bear," Luke said.

Memories of how Sam's body had been mauled rose before her. "No. Don't put yourself in danger. It's not worth it." She grabbed his arm to keep him from moving. "Please, Luke. I couldn't bear it if anything happened to you."

"I couldn't *bear* it, either," he said with a grin. "I'll be careful, Abby. Don't worry about me. Besides, I've got my gun if anything goes wrong." He didn't have to tell her he would shoot to kill if it became necessary. "Once I have the grizzly distracted, you can tranquilize the wolf."

Abigail's heart was in her throat as Luke moved off into the underbrush. She had no idea how he planned to distract the bear, but she was horrified when she saw him come up behind the bear and jab it with a tree branch.

The bear turned to confront its new tormentor with a roar. Luke quickly retreated, but the wolf took advantage of the opportunity to attack the bear from the rear, and the grizzly turned back once again to its four-legged nemesis.

"Luke," Abigail shouted. "Forget it. We'll come back later."

"No. This will work." He jabbed again, and this time the bear took several steps toward him. When it did, Abigail distracted the wolf by showing herself.

"Hello, there, you beautiful renegade, you," she said. The wolf was paralyzed for an instant as their eyes locked, green to gold.

Luke poked at the yearling grizzly's

nose, to which the beast took great exception.

When the grizzly went up on its hind legs, Abigail forgot all about the wolf, awed by the fearsome sight of the bear which, while still far from grown, was nevertheless an impressive foe. She immediately raised her tranquilizer gun to shoot the grizzly, as Luke slowly, carefully, backed away from the towering beast.

Before Abigail could fire, the unexpected happened. The wolf abruptly attacked the towering bear from behind. Startled, the grizzly dropped down on all fours to flee—straight toward Luke. Luke didn't have time to back up, or even to turn and run, before the bear was on him.

Abigail didn't stop to think, she just ran toward Luke, shouting at the top of her lungs, her only thought to save him, even at the cost of her own life. Her advance caused the pups to retreat inside the den and the mother wolf to flee. The grizzly heard the noise behind it and turned, rising once more on two legs. Abigail stared up at the bear's terrifying jaws, frozen with fear.

"Don't move, Abby," Luke said in a quiet voice. "Don't move an inch."

"I'm all right, Luke. I'm going to use the tranquilizer gun. I can't miss. He'll be out like a light in a very few minutes." She took a deep calming breath. She knew how long *a few minutes* could be. "If he isn't," she continued, "I expect you to come to the rescue."

Luke knew Abigail had a better chance with the tranquilizer gun than he did with a bullet. He might not kill the bear with his first shot, and an enraged grizzly would be infinitely more dangerous.

Abigail slowly raised the gun to her shoulder, took aim and fired.

The grizzly dropped on all fours when the dart hit him. At the same moment, Luke prodded him from behind again, and the grizzly pivoted and headed toward Luke.

Luke backed up slowly, letting the bear come toward him. Abigail's aim had been true. They took turns baiting the bear for the few hazardous minutes until the dart took effect. At long last, the grizzly staggered and fell.

Luke edged around the bear and came running toward Abby, who was still standing in front of the wolf den. He pulled her into his arms and held her tight. "Are you all right? You're not hurt?"

"I'm fine. What about you?" Abigail was still clutching her tranquilizer gun but frantically ran her free hand over Luke, making sure he hadn't been hurt.

"I'm fine, thanks to you. You could have been killed pulling a stunt like that! Whatever possessed you to do something so crazy?" he demanded.

"Look who's talking!" She hung on to her anger because it was all that kept her from crying with relief. "I've never heard of anything so idiotic as baiting a bear like that."

"It worked, didn't it?"

"What if it hadn't? You'd be dead, and I'd be heartbroken!" She realized that her worst fear had almost been realized...again. "Oh, Luke. You could have been killed!"

Luke pulled her into his arms. In her agitation she had said that losing him would leave her *heartbroken*. He was certain she hadn't meant to reveal so much. Yet Luke didn't remark on her words for fear she would deny their significance. He merely calmed her by saying, "I'm fine, Abby. I'm okay."

All he could think, as he held her in his arms, was how his heart had frozen when he'd seen her come running toward both wolf and grizzly, risking her life to save his.

He opened his mouth to say I love you and shut it again. People said things, felt things, in moments of crisis that weren't real. This was one of those times when it would be better to wait before speaking.

So he didn't say what he was thinking. He merely held her until her trembling stopped, and said, "You realize, of course, that you've scared off the wolf you came here to catch."

"She'll be back," Abigail said with certainty. "She's not going to abandon her pups. And we'll be waiting. It's only a matter of time now. That renegade is as good as trapped."

Luke had the uncomfortable feeling she could have said the same thing about him.

She'd captured his heart, and with it, his mind and soul. If she left him, *when* she left him, she would take them with her. He'd been lonely before she came into his life. He'd be devastated when she was gone. Yet he couldn't bring himself to say the words that would keep her with him.

"I'll take the wolves to a relocation area in Glacier National Park and collar the female there," Abigail explained, as though she already had the renegade caged. "Then I'll be heading back to Helena. I want to thank you for all your help."

Luke stared at the hand she held out to him and then looked into her solemn green eyes. She hadn't forgiven him for last night. And she was denying—by ignoring—the words of love she'd so recently uttered. Apparently, she was going to leave with things still unsettled between them.

Like hell she was!

"We have some unfinished business before you go anywhere," he said in a rough voice.

"Oh? Like what?"

Luke's fisted hands landed on his hips.

"Like maybe you're carrying my baby inside you right now, that's what!"

Abigail's hand slipped down to cover her womb. She'd known it was the right time of month for her to get pregnant. She had no explanation for why she hadn't stopped Luke to make sure she was protected. Except she'd been certain he was going to let her walk out of his life, and if this was all she could have of him she'd been determined to take it.

"Are you suggesting we get married because I might be pregnant?" Abigail asked.

Luke stared at her, opened his mouth to say the words, and then couldn't get them out. It was why his parents had married, and their marriage had been a disaster. "That's not a good reason for two people to marry."

"I agree," Abigail said with a sad smile. "People should marry because they love each other and want to spend their lives together—two halves, making one perfect whole."

She was leaving it up to him. All he had to say was three words, and he could take her home and spend the rest of his life with her.

"I'm sorry, Abby. I don't think I can love anybody," Luke confessed, his voice laced with regret.

"You're wrong, Luke. But I guess you'll have to find that out for yourself. If you do, *when you do,* you know where to find me."

She turned and walked away. She wasn't going far, just to collect the equipment they needed to set up camp. But she might as well have been headed for Timbuktu, he felt such a sense of loss.

Because she'd already taken the first steps out of his life.

10

Wolves mate for life.

Luke and Abigail hauled the unconscious bear some distance away from the wolf den and watched to make sure the grizzly wasn't attacked by some other forest animal before it regained consciousness. Once they were sure the bear was on its feet again, they returned to the wolf den.

Not far from the opening of the den they found the remains of the three-toed wolf's mate. There was a bullet hole in the gray wolf's hide. Apparently the male wolf had come back here to die. Abigail exchanged a poignant glance at Luke.

"I didn't shoot him, Abby."

"Somebody did."

"I can't deny that. I can even make a pretty good guess how it happened. There's a lot of misunderstanding about wolves out there, Abby. You certainly have your work cut out for you.''

Abigail turned sad eyes on Luke. ''I only hope that what I'm doing will make a difference.''

''It will,'' Luke assured her, taking her hands in his.

Luke's touch was comforting, but it reminded her of all she would soon be denied. She broke away and said, ''We'd better find a place to conceal ourselves. That she-wolf won't come back until she thinks we're gone.''

As Abigail had predicted, late in the afternoon the renegade returned to her pups. From a hiding place downwind, Abigail was able to dart the wolf with the tranquilizer gun, and while it was unconscious, cage it in the collapsible wire cage, much like a dog traveling cage, she'd brought along. The pups were still small enough that Abigail merely used gloves and slipped them into the cage with their mother.

Abigail had counted on having to carry the cage with the hundred-pound wolf back down the mountain, but the extra weight of the pups was going to complicate matters. She was trying to figure out the best way to distribute the weight of the animals between them when Luke pulled out a portable phone and began dialing.

"What are you doing?"

"Getting us a ride home." He contacted the closest rancher and asked him to phone Shorty, giving him directions where to meet them. Then he tucked the phone back into his bag again. "You look surprised," he said to Abby.

"I am. And pleased," Abigail added with a rueful smile. "I should have thought of that myself. I sure wasn't looking forward to hauling that she-wolf and her pups all the way down the mountain."

"It'll be a long enough hike to get to the road," Luke said.

As quickly as that, they ran out of things to say to each other. Abigail stared for a moment, then turned away and busied herself packing up the last of her equipment, which she hefted onto her back. They ran a pole through the cage to provide an easier means of distributing the wolves' weight. Fortunately the walk to the road, while grueling, was short.

As they sat waiting by the side of the road for Shorty to arrive, the silence became oppressive.

When Abigail couldn't stand the quiet tension any longer she asked, "How does Shorty know where to pick us up?"

"I told him to come to the spot where we killed the timber rattler last summer."

Abigail quickly lifted her feet and looked around the ground under the dead log on which she was perched. "Are there a lot of snakes up here?"

"Enough. It's a little early in the season for them to be active, though."

Once again, the silence descended.

Abigail wanted to ask whether she was going to see Luke again, and whether he thought there was any chance for a future between the two of them. But Luke had already made his feelings plain. She wasn't going to get a different answer simply by asking him again.

Luke chewed on his lower lip, wondering

if he was making a big mistake letting Abby walk out of his life. The more he thought about it, the more he thought that what had happened between them must simply have been born out of the unique situation into which they'd been thrust together. He'd known the woman for less than a week! Surely a love that was meant to last a lifetime took longer than that to take seed and grow. Thanks to his foolishness, however, there was another seed that might take root and grow.

He cleared his throat and said, "If you find out—if you're…if there's a baby, I expect you to call me."

Abigail had her knees tucked up to her chest, with her arms hugging them. "If I'm pregnant, it'll be my business and not yours."

"Like hell it will!" Luke said, grabbing Abigail by the arm and yanking her to her feet. "If you're pregnant, that child is mine, too. I'll be part of the decision—"

"We've already agreed it would be foolish to get married because of a baby, Luke," Abigail said, trying to reason with him. "I don't see what purpose it would serve to—"

"Nobody's killing another child of mine!" he snarled.

Abby stared at him in horror. "Is that what you think? That if I were pregnant with your child, I'd get rid of it?"

"Wouldn't you?" he challenged, his voice cold and hard with fury.

As his wife had done, she suddenly realized. Her heart went out to him for the pain he'd suffered in the past. How could any woman have hurt him so much?

"I love you, Luke. I know you don't believe me or understand what that means, but it's true. I would love a baby we made together. I could never kill it."

He wanted to call her a liar. All women were liars. They only said what they thought a man wanted to hear. Except, what Luke saw in Abby's deep green eyes was honesty. What he heard in her voice was sincerity. Confused, he let go of her and stalked away.

Abby sat down on the log again, rubbing her arms where Luke had held her in anger.

He paced back and forth in front of the log like a caged animal, never coming to rest.

Abigail saw his distress but had no idea how to pacify the savage beast in him. "I owe you a great deal, Luke," she said at last.

"For what?" he said, halting in front of her.

"For showing me that I don't have to be afraid of loving again. That it's better to have loved and lost, than never to have loved at all."

Luke snorted. "Hogwash."

"We'll see," she said.

"What's that supposed to mean?"

"That I'm not sorry for loving you, even if you can't love me back. That I don't regret this time with you, even if I can't have more. Not that I don't wish for more," she said wistfully.

"Be honest, Abby," Luke said, putting his foot up on the log beside her and, bracing his arm on his thigh, knowing he was crowding her. "All we had going for us was damned good sex."

Abigail shook her head sadly. "It was much more than that, Luke. Maybe the reason you don't recognize what we had together is because you've never been in love—really in love—before. But I have."

"With Sam the Magnificent."

"With Sam," she continued doggedly. "What I feel for you is so much more, so much greater, than what I felt for him, that I know it can't be a lie."

She would have said more except the honking of a truck horn—Shorty in Luke's pickup—interrupted her.

Abigail had thrown caution to the winds. She'd spoken from the heart. What Luke chose to do with that information was anybody's guess. She was expecting heartache, and he didn't disappoint her.

"All I want from you," he said, talking quickly to get everything said before Shorty arrived, "is a promise that you'll call me if you find out you're carrying my child. That's all. Nothing else. Do you understand?"

"Yes, Luke," Abigail said in a quiet voice. "I understand all too well."

"So you'll call me."

"No, Luke, I won't. It's going to be painful enough to leave you. I won't let you back into my life to hurt me again."

"Damn it, Abby, I—"

"Hey, Luke, Miss Abigail. You two ready for a ride?" Shorty yelled.

Luke swore loudly and creatively as he grabbed his and Abigail's bags and slung them into the back of the pickup. He removed the carrying pole and loaded it, then hefted the cage with the wolf and her pups onto the tailgate and shoved it onto the bed of the pickup, daring Abigail to help him.

Abigail stood and watched, angry with the stubborn man who refused to admit he loved her—because she felt sure he did. Well, she wasn't going to go into a decline and die when she left him behind. She'd picked up the pieces before and kept on living. She could do it again.

Shorty saw from the body language between Luke and Miss Abigail that the romance he'd hoped was budding between them had come to naught. He was sorry for that. Shorty did his best to keep a conver-

sation going on the drive away down the
mountain, but it was clear the two of them
were pretty distracted.

He caught a couple of searing looks between them that gave him some hope that
all was not lost. If the two of them were
having this much trouble leaving each
other, time apart might allow them to re-
consider. He was willing to bide his time.
Meanwhile, he'd be sure to provide Luke
with lots of reminders of his time with Miss
Abigail.

After the wolves and Abigail's equipment had been reloaded onto her own truck,
she gave Shorty a quick buss on the cheek
goodbye. Then she turned to Luke and said,
"Thank you again…for everything."

Luke wanted to pull her into his arms, to
hold her tight, to kiss her, to thrust himself
inside her and make them one. *He wanted
to keep her with him.* That thought frightened him so much that he said a curt,
"Goodbye, Abby," pivoted on a booted
heel and stalked off.

Tears welled in Abigail's eyes as she
watched him walk away. Realizing that

Shorty was watching, she dabbed at her eyes with her sleeve and said, "Thanks again, Shorty." Then she turned and ran to her truck. Gunning the engine, she raced down the dirt and gravel drive.

"Be seein' you," Shorty yelled after her. He turned and squinted an eye in the direction Luke had retreated. "I do believe I'll be seein' ya."

Abigail made one stop before heading home. When she drove up to Harry Alistair's tiny log cabin she saw that numerous improvements had been made in the condition of the property. Harry was out in the pigpen again, and as Abigail walked up, Harry left it through the gate, which had been repaired.

"I came to say goodbye," Abigail said. "And to see how you're doing. It looks like things have changed around here for the better."

"Come on up to the house for a cup of coffee," Harry said, taking off her cap and wiping her brow with her sleeve, "and I'll tell you all about it."

"I can only stay a few minutes," Abigail said. "I need to get these wolves back to Helena tonight." She gestured toward the wolf and her pups, which were in the back of the pickup.

Harry came over to admire them. "She's beautiful. They're all beautiful. Where will you take them?"

"There are already some breeding pairs in the Bob Marshall Wilderness in Glacier National Park. After she's radio-tagged, I'll look for a place with good water and rendezvous spots for her pups and leave her there."

Abigail looked around at all the changes for the better in Harry's property. "I'm dying of curiosity, Harry. How did you manage all these improvements so fast?"

Harry pulled off her gloves and leaned a hip against the fender of Abigail's pickup. "I've got a new ranch manager—Nathan Hazard," she said bitterly.

"You don't sound too happy about it," Abigail noted.

"Would you be happy if help was forced down your throat?" Harry said. "I needed a loan from the bank because—well, because I had a little cash-flow problem. John Wilkinson at the bank wouldn't make the loan unless Nathan Hazard agreed to help me manage my place. Said otherwise I was too much of a credit risk.''

''Won't this arrangement give you a chance to learn what you need to know to get along on your own?'' Abigail asked.

''You bet it will! The day I sell my crop of lambs and pay off that loan, is the day I see the backside of Nathan Hazard for good.''

Privately Abigail thought Harry seemed a little more upset than the situation warranted. But maybe there was more going on between Nathan and Harry than met the eye. ''I wish you luck, Harry,'' Abigail said, extending her hand for the other woman to shake.

''Thanks, Abby,'' Harry said, grasping Abigail's hand in hers and pumping it twice. ''It means a lot to me to have you for a friend. If there's ever anything I can do to help you out, give me a call.''

''I might just do that,'' Abigail replied.

"Meanwhile," she said, "make sure you don't leave any wolf bait lying around."

"You got it," Harry said, returning Abby's smile. "So long, Abby."

Luke had thought he knew what it was like to live with a broken heart. That was before he fell in love with Abby and let her walk out of his life. More like chased her out of his life, he admitted.

Here he was, six weeks later, standing on the darkened doorstep to her wood-frame house in a quiet residential section of Helena, working up the courage to ring the doorbell and ask her to be his wife. He had never been more afraid of anything in his life.

What if she says no?

Luke rang the bell twice, but there was no answer. He looked in through the lace-curtained window, and saw there was a light on in the kitchen. She had to be there. The phone had been busy when he'd tried to call from her office and let her know he was coming. Her boss had said she had gone home sick.

Luke didn't want to think what that might mean. After all the things he'd said, if she did turn out to be pregnant, it was going to be even harder to convince her to marry him. Not that he would let that stand in his way.

He leaned against the bell and let it ring. If she was in there, he wasn't going to allow her to ignore him.

Abigail was on the phone with a rancher in Kalispell who had sighted a pair of wolves and was worried about his stock. She ignored the doorbell because she wasn't expecting anyone, and because she hated door-to-door salesmen. But the constant ringing didn't stop.

"Could you hold on just a moment," she said to the rancher on the phone. "I'll be right back."

She ran to the door and threw it open, prepared to lambaste the party at the door. She was astonished to find Luke Granger standing there, hat in hand.

"Your boss said you came home sick," Luke said. "Why aren't you in bed?"

"It was only an upset stomach," she replied.

Luke's eyes narrowed and dropped to her belly.

Abigail's hand protectively covered her womb. "What are you doing here, Luke?"

"I want to talk to you. Let me in."

"I think we've said everything we have to say to one another." She tried closing the door.

A second later he was inside with the door shut behind him.

Abigail backed away from him. "I'm busy, Luke."

"You don't look busy to me," he said, his eyes roaming over her from head to foot and back again. He'd been starved for the sight of her and couldn't get enough of looking at her. She hadn't been getting enough sleep. There were dark circles under her eyes. And she'd lost weight. She couldn't afford to get any thinner. She needed to eat if she was pregnant. *Pregnant.* He swallowed hard. Was she?

Abigail felt uncomfortable under Luke's perusing gaze. But she was looking, too.

His cheeks were even more hollow than before. He didn't look well. Or happy. Why had he come? Why didn't he speak? "I was talking to someone on the phone," she said, heading back toward the kitchen. "If you'll wait—"

Luke was right behind her as she picked up the phone.

"Hello, Harley," she said. "Just someone at the door."

"Who's Harley?" Luke demanded. While he'd been going out of his mind without her, it sounded like she'd already found another boyfriend!

"Excuse me a minute, Harley," Abby said. She put the phone against her chest to muffle the sound and hissed, "Who I talk to is none of your business, Luke Granger. Now, I'll thank you to—"

Luke took the phone out of her hand and said, "Who the hell is this?"

"Harley Frederickson," a surly voice answered. "Who the hell is this? I got wolf trouble, and I need help. Put Abby back on the phone."

"Agent Dayton's got some wolf trouble

of her own to deal with first,'' Luke responded, never taking his eyes off Abby. ''She'll call you back tomorrow.''

Luke hung up the phone and leaned a hip against the kitchen counter.

''That is the most high-handed—''

Luke pulled her into his arms and kissed her. It was a kiss that said *I love you and I need you.* Abby was breathless when he finally released her.

''Are you pregnant?'' he asked.

''That is none of your—''

He kissed her again, in case she hadn't gotten the message. *I love you. I want to make babies with you. I want us to spend our lives together.* Only he thought the words, he didn't say them.

''Are you pregnant?'' he asked again, his voice husky with feeling.

Abigail searched his eyes. She didn't want the baby to make a difference. She didn't want a marriage he would come to regret. ''What if I am?''

''We'll get married.'' Luke knew immediately, when her body stiffened in his arms, that he'd said the wrong thing. ''Aw, hell, Abby," he said, releasing her and forking a hand through his hair. "That came out all wrong. That isn't why I came here. The baby, I mean. If there is a baby, I mean. Aw, hell."

Abigail found hope in his confusion. "Why did you come here, Luke?"

"I came because I need you like I need water to drink and sunshine on my face and the sight of the mountains at daybreak. I can't live without you, Abby. I want you to be my wife."

It was the longest declaration of love Luke had ever made to a woman in his life. His pulse was galloping when he was finished. He'd put his heart in her hands. It was in her power to crush it.

"Oh, Luke," Abigail said, as a single tear slipped onto her cheek.

"Is that a yes or a no?" he croaked.

She took a step into his open arms and grasped him tightly around the waist. "That's yes. Yes, I love you. Yes, I'll be your wife. Yes, I'll be the mother of your children."

Luke kissed her then, and neither of them

said anything for a good long while. Until Luke remembered that she'd never said for sure whether or not she was pregnant.

"Uh, Abby—about the baby…"

"Yes, Luke?"

"Yes?"

"I'm pregnant." Abby didn't have to see Luke's face. She could feel his reaction. His whole body tensed before his arms tightened around her.

"I'm glad," he whispered. "I'm so glad."

"What made you change your mind, Luke?" Abigail whispered as she held him close, loving the feel of being held in his arms.

Luke chuckled. "I'm sure Shorty will take the credit."

"Oh? What did he say?"

"That if I wasn't as dumb as the sheep I raised, I'd make you my wife."

Abigail laughed. "Good advice."

"And Nathan's sure to claim he's the one who brought about my change of heart."

"Nathan?"

"He said if I didn't come here and propose to you, he was going to do it for me."

Abigail laughed. "I take it you haven't been the easiest man to be around lately."

"You might say that," he agreed. "By the way, I promised Nathan he could be my best man."

"Oh, dear."

"Some problem with that?"

"I thought I'd ask Harry to be my maid of honor."

Luke smiled down into Abby's mischievous green eyes. "That's going to ensure an eventful wedding."

"You're avoiding my question," Abigail said. "What made you change your mind?"

"I love you, Abby." It was amazing how right the words sounded, now that he'd actually spoken them aloud. "Once I admitted that to myself, everything fell into place. I knew I would never be happy unless you were part of my life."

The kiss came naturally, out of feelings that rose up from deep inside him.

Abigail was moved by his gentleness, aroused by his ferocity. She began undoing the buttons on Luke's chambray shirt. "What are your neighbors going to think when they find out you're marrying a woman who's devoted to saving wolves?"

Luke grinned. "I don't know about them, but I'd say when it comes to catching renegades, you really know your business."

"I hope you know I don't ever intend to let you go."

"I sort of expected that."

"Oh?" she asked, as her lips teased his.

"I read somewhere that wolves mate for life. Is that true, Abby?"

"Oh, yes," she sighed. "They mate forever and ever and—"

He didn't give her a chance to say more, just joined her mouth with his, telling her of his love in the most elemental way. Still, he might have considered howling with joy—if his mouth hadn't been otherwise delightfully occupied.

*   *   *   *   *

Secrets, lies, blame and guilt.
Only love and forgiveness can overcome
the mistakes of the past.

Rachel Lee

Witt Matlock has carried around a bitter hatred for Hardy
Wingate, the man he holds responsible for the death of his
daughter. And now, twelve years later, the man he blames for
the tragedy is back in his life—and in that of his niece, Joni.

Widow Hannah Matlock has kept the truth about her
daughter Joni's birth hidden for twenty-seven years. Only she
knows that her brother-in-law Witt is Joni's father, and not
her uncle. But with Hardy coming between Witt and Joni,
Hannah knows she must let go of her secret...whatever the
consequences.

A January Chill

On sale April 2001 wherever paperbacks are sold!

MIRA®

JOAN
JOHNSTON

66629   A LITTLE TIME IN TEXAS   ___ $5.99 U.S. ___ $6.99 CAN.

(limited quantities available)

TOTAL AMOUNT	$_____
POSTAGE & HANDLING	$_____
($1.00 for one book; 50¢ for each additional)	
APPLICABLE TAXES*	$_____
TOTAL PAYABLE	$_____

(check or money order—please do not send cash)

To order, complete this form and send it, along with a check or money order for the total above, payable to MIRA Books®, to: **In the U.S.:** 3010 Walden Avenue, P.O. Box 9077, Buffalo, NY 14269-9077; **In Canada:** P.O. Box 636, Fort Erie, Ontario L2A 5X3.

Name:_____

Address:_____ City:_____

State/Prov.:_____ Zip/Postal Code:_____

Account Number (if applicable):_____

075 CSAS

MIRA®